ALSO BY JENNY OFFILL

Last Things

DEPT. OF SPECULATION

DEPT. OF SPECULATION

JENNY OFFILL

Alfred A. Knopf New York 2015

THIS IS A BORZOI BOOK
PUBLISHED BY ALFRED A. KNOPF

www.aaknopf.com

Knopf, Borzoi Books, and the colophon are registered trademarks of
Random House LLC.

Portions of this work first appeared, in slightly different form, in
the following: moistworks.com (March 2007); significantobjects.com
(March 2010); Significant Objects: 100 Extraordinary Stories
About Ordinary Things, edited by Joshua Glenn and Rob Walker
(Seattle: Fantagraphics, 2012); Tin House (December 2013); and
The Paris Review (December 2013).

Library of Congress Cataloging-in-Publication Data
Offill, Jenny, 1968–
Dept. of speculation / Jenny Offill.
pages cm
ISBN 978-0-385-35081-5
1. Marriage—Fiction. 2. Family life—Fiction. 3. Domestic fiction.
4. Psychological fiction. I. Title. II. Title: Department of speculation.
PS3565.F383D47 2014
813'.54—dc23   2013019367

Jacket design and illustration by Joan Wong

Manufactured in the United States of America
Published January 14, 2014
Second Printing, January 2015

FOR DAVE

Speculators on the universe . . .
are no better than madmen.

—SOCRATES

DEPT. OF SPECULATION

1

Antelopes have 10× vision, you said. It was the beginning or close to it. That means that on a clear night they can see the rings of Saturn.

It was still months before we'd tell each other all our stories. And even then some seemed too small to bother with. So why do they come back to me now? Now, when I'm so weary of all of it.

Memories are microscopic. Tiny particles that swarm together and apart. Little people, Edison called them. Entities. He had a theory about where they came from and that theory was outer space.

The first time I traveled alone, I went to a restaurant and ordered a steak. But when it came I saw it was just a piece of raw meat cut into pieces. I tried to eat it, but it was too bloody. My throat refused to swallow. Finally, I spit it out into a napkin. There was still a great deal of meat on my plate. I was afraid the waiter would notice I wasn't eating and laugh or yell at me. For a long time, I sat there, looking at it. Then I took a roll, hollowed it out, and secreted the meat inside it. I had a very small purse but I thought I could fit the roll in without being seen. I paid the bill, and walked out, expecting to be stopped, but no one stopped me.

I spent my afternoons in a city park, pretending to read Horace. At dusk, people streamed out of the Métro and into the street. In Paris, even the subways are required to be beautiful. *They change their sky, not their soul, who run across the sea.*

There was a Canadian boy who ate only oatmeal. A French boy who asked to examine my teeth. An English boy who came from a line of druids. A Dutch boy who sold hearing aids.

I met an Australian who said he loved to travel alone. He talked about his job as we drank by the sea. When a student gets it, when it first breaks across his face, it's so fucking beautiful, he told me. I nodded, moved, though I'd never taught anyone a single thing. What do you teach, I asked him. Rollerblading, he explained.

That was the summer it rained and rained. I remember the sad doggish smell of my sweater and my shoes sloshing crazily. And in every city, the same scene. A boy stepping into the street and opening an umbrella for a girl keeping dry in the doorway.

Another night. My old apartment in Brooklyn. It was late, but of course, I couldn't sleep. Above me, speed freaks merrily disassembling something. Leaves against the window. I felt a sudden chill and pulled the blanket over my head. That's the way they bring horses out of a fire, I remembered. If they can't see, they won't panic. I tried to figure out if I felt calmer with a blanket over my head. No I did not was the answer.

2

I got a job checking facts at a science magazine. Fun facts, they called them. *The connected fibers in a human brain, extended, would wrap around the Earth forty times.* Horrible, I wrote in the margin, but they put it through anyway.

I liked my apartment because all of the windows were at street level. In the summer, I could see people's shoes, and in the winter, snow. Once, as I lay in bed, a bright red sun appeared in the window. It bounced from side to side, then became a ball.

Life equals structure plus activity.

Studies suggest that reading makes enormous demands on the neurological system. One psychiatric journal claimed that African tribes needed more sleep after being taught to read. The French were great believers in such theories. During World War II, the largest rations went to those engaged in arduous physical labor and those whose work involved reading and writing.

For years, I kept a Post-it note above my desk. WORK NOT LOVE! was what it said. It seemed a sturdier kind of happiness.

I found a book called *Thriving Not Surviving* in a box on the street. I stood there, flipping through it, unwilling to commit.

You think that the mental anguish you are experiencing is a permanent condition, but for the vast majority of people it is only a temporary state.

(But what if I'm special? What if I'm in the *minority?*)

I had ideas about myself. Largely untested. When I was a child, I liked to write my name in giant letters made of sticks.

What Coleridge said: *If I do not greatly delude myself, I have not only completely extricated the notions of time, and space . . . but I trust that I am about to do more—namely that I shall be able to evolve all the five senses . . . & in this evolvement to solve the process of life and consciousness.*

My plan was to never get married. I was going to be an art monster instead. Women almost never become art monsters because art monsters only concern themselves with art, never mundane things. Nabokov didn't even fold his own umbrella. Vera licked his stamps for him.

A bold plan was what my friend, the philosopher, said. But on my twenty-ninth birthday I turned my book in. *If I do not greatly delude myself . . .*

I went to a party and drank myself sick.

Are animals lonely?
Other animals, I mean.

Not long after that, an ex-boyfriend appeared on my doorstep. He seemed to have come all

the way from San Francisco just to have coffee. On the way to the diner, he apologized
for never really loving me. He hoped to make
amends. "Wait," I said. "Are you doing the
steps?"

That night on TV, I saw the tattoo I wished
my life had warranted. *If you have not known
suffering, love me.* A Russian murderer beat
me to it.

Of course, I thought of the drunkard boy in
New Orleans, the one I loved best. Each night
at the old sailors' bar, I'd peel the labels off
his bottles and try to entice him homeward.
But he wouldn't come. Not until light came
through the window.

That one was so beautiful I used to watch him
sleep. If I had to sum up what he did to me,
I'd say it was this: he made me sing along to
all the bad songs on the radio. Both when he
loved me and when he didn't.

In those last weeks, we drove without talking, trying to outride the heat, each alone in the dream the city had become. I was afraid to speak, to touch his arm even. *Remember this sign, this tree, this broken-down street. Remember it is possible to feel this way.* There were twenty days on the calendar, then fifteen, then ten, then the day I packed my car and left. I drove the length of two states, sobbing, heat like a hand against my chest. But I didn't. I didn't remember it.

3

There is a man who travels around the world trying to find places where you can stand still and hear no human sound. It is impossible to feel calm in cities, he believes, because we so rarely hear birdsong there. Our ears evolved to be our warning systems. We are on high alert in places where no birds sing. To live in a city is to be forever flinching.

The Buddhists say there are 121 states of consciousness. Of these, only three involve misery or suffering. Most of us spend our time moving back and forth between these three.

Blue jays spend every Friday with the devil, the old lady at the park told me.

"You need to get out of that stupid city," my sister said. "Get some fresh air." Four years ago, she and her husband left. They moved to Pennsylvania to an old ramshackle house on the Delaware River. Last spring, she came to visit me with her kids. We went to the park; we went to the zoo; we went to the planetarium. But still they hated it. *Why is everyone yelling here?*

The philosopher's apartment was the most peaceful place I knew. It had good light and looked out over the water. We spent our Sundays there eating pancakes and eggs. He was adjuncting now and doing late nights at the radio station. "You should meet this guy I work with. He makes soundscapes of the city." I looked at the pigeons outside his window. "What does that even mean?" I said.

He gave me a CD to take home. On the cover was an old yellow phone book, ruined by rain. I closed my eyes and listened to it. Who is this person? I wondered.

4

I gave you my favorite thing from China-
town, pressed it drunkenly into your hand.
We were in my kitchen that first night.
BEAUTIFUL GAUZE MASK, the package said.

The next morning, I went over to the philosopher's apartment. "Oh no, what have you
done?" I said. He made me breakfast and told
me about his date. "Where do you see yourself in five years?" she'd asked him. "How
about ten? How about fifteen?" By the time
he walked her home, they were thirty years
in. I told him it sounded like a duck and a bear
going on a date. The philosopher considered
this. "More like a duck and a martini," he said.

You called me. I called you. *Come over, come
over*, we said.

I learned you were fearless about the weather.
You wanted to walk around the city, come

rain come snow come sleet, recording things. I bought a warmer coat with many ingenious pockets. You put your hands in all of them.

I listened to you on the radio at midnight. Once you played a recording of atoms smashing. Another time wind across leaves. Field recordings, you called them. It was freezing in my apartment and I used to listen to your show in bed with the covers pulled up to my chin. I wore a hat and gloves and heavy wool socks made for men. One night you played a track you'd made for me. An ice cream truck overlaid with the sound of gulls at Coney Island and the Wonder Wheel spinning.

It is stupid to have a telescope in the city, but we bought one anyway.

That year I didn't travel alone. I'll meet you there, you said. But it was late when we spotted each other at the train station. You had a ten-dollar haircut. I was fatter than when I'd left. It seemed possible that we'd traveled across the world in error. We tried to reserve judgment.

We did not understand where we were going when we took the boat over to Capri. It was early April. A light cold rain misted over the sea. We took a funicular up from the dock and found ourselves the only tourists. You are early, the conductor said with a shrug. The streets smelled like lavender and for a long time neither of us noticed that there weren't any cars. We stayed at a cheap hotel that had a view out the window more beautiful than anything I'd ever seen. The water was wickedly blue. A cliff of dark rock jutted out of the sea. I wanted to cry because I was sure I would never get to be in such a place again. Let's explore, you said, which is what you always said when I started to look that way. We walked for a ways along the edge of the cliff until we came to a bus stop. There we waited, holding hands, not talking. I was thinking about what it would be like to live somewhere so beautiful. Would it fix my brain? The bus pulled up. Three people were employed to run it: one to sell tickets, one to take them, one to drive. This made us happy. We took it to the far side of the island, where the people looked more curiously at us. In a store, I saw gum labeled BROOKLYN and you bought it for me.

5

We passed the antelope diorama. "10×," I said, but you wouldn't look at me. "What's the matter?" I asked. Nothing. Nothing. But, later, in the gem room, you got down on one knee. All around us shining things.

Advice from Hesiod: *Choose from among the girls who live near you and check every detail, so that your bride will not be the neighborhood joke. Nothing is better for man than a good wife, and no horror matches a bad one.*

Afterwards, we ducked into the borrowed room, fell back onto the borrowed bed. Outside, almost everyone who'd ever loved us waited. You took my hand, kissed it, saying, "What have we done? What the hell have we done?"

When we first met, I had a persistent cough. A smoker's cough, though I'd never smoked.

I went from doctor to doctor, but no one ever fixed it. In those early days, I spent a great deal of energy trying not to cough so much. I would lie awake next to you at night and try my best not to. I had an idea that I might have contracted TB. *Here lies one whose name was writ in water,* I thought pleasingly. But no, that wasn't it either. Just after we married, the cough went away. So what was it, I wonder?

Loneliness?

Lying in bed, you'd cradle my skull as if there were a soft spot there that needed to be protected. *Stay close to me,* you'd say. *Why are you way over there?*

The reason to have a home is to keep certain people in and everyone else out. A home has a perimeter. But sometimes our perimeter was breached by neighbors, by Girl Scouts, by Jehovah's Witnesses. I never liked to hear the doorbell ring. None of the people I liked ever turned up that way.

Also there were incursions from within. Mice, mice, everywhere. We borrowed a cat for a month, a ferocious mouser, who caught and ate all of them. His name was Carl and I could hear him up all night crunching their bones in the kitchen. It gave me a bad feeling, worse than the scuttling of the mice even. The boy I'd loved in New Orleans had told me once that his father used to kill mice by dropping them in boiling water. I was too surprised to ask then how he'd caught the mice or why he killed them that way, but later I wondered. His father was from another country so maybe that was how they did things over there.

In my old apartment, the mice had cavorted even more openly. They had no fear, not of light or even brooms, it seemed. They lived in my pantry and one night while we were lying in bed, the door fell off its hinges and thudded to the floor. "I think they saved up for that battering ram," you said.

6

His mother was visiting when we went to look at the apartment. She pointed out the church across the street. It pleased her that you could see Jesus on the cross if you leaned a little out the window. This was a good sign, she thought, and was not canceled out by the fact that her son no longer believed in him.

When we first saw the apartment, we were excited that it had a yard but disappointed that the yard was filled by a large jungle gym that we didn't need. Later, when we signed the lease, we were happy about the jungle gym because I'd learned that I was pregnant and we could imagine its uses. But by the time we moved in, we had found out that the baby's heart had stopped and now it just made us sad to look out the window at it.

I remember that day, how you took a $50 cab from work, how you held me in the doorway until I stopped shaking. We had told people. We had to untell them. You did it so I wouldn't have to speak. Later, you made me a dinner of all the things I hadn't been allowed to eat. Cured meat, unpasteurized cheese. Two bottles of wine, then finally, sleep.

I fed the birds outside my window. Sparrows, I believed them to be.

Q. Is the sparrow a native of this country?

A. It is now, but not long ago there were no sparrows in America.

Q. Why were the sparrows brought to this country?

A. Because the insects were killing so many trees that the sparrows were needed to destroy the insects.

Q. Did the sparrows save the trees?

A. Yes, the trees were saved.

Q. In wintertime when there are no insects and snow is on the ground, does not the sparrow have a hard time?

A. Yes, he has a very hard time, and many die of hunger.

The woman with the white hair and the mustache always held up the line at Rite Aid. Sometimes I waited fifteen minutes just to buy my antacids. Ever since I'd gotten pregnant again, I'd gobbled up a pack a day. But my big belly never swayed her. She would not be hurried. One afternoon I watched as she presented her items one by one to the handsome young clerk.

"You're lucky," she said to him. "You still have it all ahead of you. My sister and I both have genius IQs. I went to Cornell. Do you know what that is?"

The clerk smiled but shook his head no.

"It's an Ivy League school. But it doesn't matter. It all comes to nothing in the end."

Carefully, he bagged her groceries. Toothpaste, itching cream, off-brand candy. "Take care of yourself," he told her when she left, but she lingered in the doorway. "When are you working again?" she asked him. "Do you have your schedule yet?"

7

The baby's eyes were dark, almost black, and when I nursed her in the middle of the night, she'd stare at me with a stunned, shipwrecked look as if my body were the island she'd washed up on.

The Manicheans believed the world was filled with imprisoned light, fragments of a God who destroyed himself because he no longer wished to exist. This light could be found trapped inside man and animals and plants, and the Manichean mission was to try to release it. Because of this, they abstained from sex, viewing babies as fresh prisons of entrapped light.

I remember the first time I said the word to a stranger. "It's for my daughter," I said. My heart was beating too fast, as if I might be arrested.

In the early days, I only ventured out of the house with her when we were desperate for food or diapers, and then I went only as far as Rite Aid. Rite Aid was a block from our apartment. It was exactly the distance I could make in the freezing cold, carrying the baby in my arms. Also the farthest distance I could sprint if she started screaming again and I had to go home. These calculations were important because she screamed a lot in those days. Enough that our neighbors averted their eyes when they saw us, enough that it felt like a car alarm was perpetually going off in my head.

After you left for work, I would stare at the door as if it might open again.

My love for her seemed doomed, hopelessly unrequited. There should be songs for this, I thought, but if there were I didn't know them.

She was small enough then to still fall asleep on your chest. Sometimes I fed you dinner with a spoon so you wouldn't have to raise your arms and wake her.

What the baby liked best was speed. If I took her outside, I had to walk quickly, even trot a little. If I slowed down or stopped, she would start wailing again. It was the dead of winter and some days I walked or trotted for hours, softly singing.

What did you do today, you'd say when you got home from work, and I'd try my best to craft an anecdote for you out of nothing.

I read a study once about sleep deprivation. The researchers made cat-sized islands of sand in the middle of a pool of water, then placed very tired cats on top of them. At first, the cats curled up perfectly on the sand and slept, but eventually they'd sprawl out and wake up in water. I can't remember what they were trying to prove exactly. All I took away was that the cats went crazy.

The days with the baby felt long but there was nothing expansive about them. Caring for her required me to repeat a series of tasks that had the peculiar quality of seeming both urgent and tedious. They cut the day up into little scraps.

And that phrase—"sleeping like a baby." Some blonde said it blithely on the subway the other day. I wanted to lie down next to her and scream for five hours in her ear.

But the smell of her hair. The way she clasped her hand around my fingers. This was like medicine. For once, I didn't have to think. The animal was ascendant.

I ordered a CD online that promised to put even the most colicky baby to sleep. It sounded like a giant heart beating. As if you had been forced to live inside such a heart with no possibility of escape.

Our friend R stopped by one night to see us while it was playing. "Wow. That is some bad techno music," he said. He sat on the couch and drank beer while I paced with the baby.

R's job involved traveling around the world, talking about the future and how we might rush towards it. I walked up and down the hall, listening to him talk to you about the end of everything. *The invention of the ship is also the invention of the shipwreck,* he was saying. Twenty steps forward, then twenty steps back again. Thump, thump, thump, thump went the music. But the heartbeat song only enraged the baby. On and on she screamed. "This is intense," R said after an hour or two. R who is not our friend anymore and began not to be on the night in question.

8

Then one day I discovered something that surprised me. The baby was calm at Rite Aid. She seemed to like the harsh light of it, the shelves of plenty. For fifteen, maybe twenty minutes, she'd suspend her fierce judgment of the world and fall silent there. And when she did, a tiny space would clear in my head and I could think again. So I began to go there with her every day, wandering up and down the narrow aisles while the terrible drugstore music played. I'd stare at the lightbulbs and the cold medicine and the mousetraps and everything looked strange and useless to me. The last time I'd felt that way I was sixteen and lived in Savannah, Georgia. I wore moth-eaten dresses and fancied myself an existentialist. The days were long then too.

We ran into the dog-walking neighbor once on our way there. He seemed to hate everything except my baby. "Serious expression," he

said approvingly. "Won't suffer fools gladly."
The baby gave him her thousand-yard stare.
She made a little sound like a growl maybe.
He wanted her to pet his dog, a giant brood-
ing mastiff with a spiked collar. "He's a good
dog," he told me. "He hates drunks and blacks
and he's not too crazy about Spanish either."

Sleep when the baby sleeps, people said. *Don't
go to bed angry.*

If I knew telekinesis, I would send this spoon
over there to feed that baby.

My best friend came to visit from far away. She
took two planes and a train to get to Brooklyn.
We met at a bar near my apartment and drank
in a hurry as the babysitter's meter ticked. In
the past, we'd talked about books and other
people, but now we talked only of our respec-
tive babies, hers sweet-faced and docile, mine
at war with the world. We applied our muzzy
intellects to a theory of light. That all are born
radiating light but that this light diminished

slowly (if one was lucky) or abruptly (if one was not). The most charismatic people—the poets, the mystics, the explorers—were that way because they had somehow managed to keep a bit of this light that was meant to have dimmed. But the shocking thing, the unbearable thing it seemed, was that the natural order was for this light to vanish. It hung on sometimes through the twenties, a glint here or there in the thirties, and then almost always the eyes went dark.

"Put a hat on that baby," said every old biddy that passed me. But the devil baby cleverly dispatched with them to ride bareheaded in the freezing rain and wind.

Is she a good baby? People would ask me. Well, no, I'd say.

That swirl of hair on the back of her head. We must have taken a thousand pictures of it.

9

He is famously kind, my husband. Always sending money to those afflicted with obscure diseases or shoveling the walk of the crazy neighbor or helloing the fat girl at Rite Aid. He's from Ohio. This means he never forgets to thank the bus driver or pushes in front at the baggage claim. Nor does he keep a list of those who infuriate him on a given day. People mean well. That is what he believes. How then is he married to me? I hate often and easily. I hate, for example, people who sit with their legs splayed. People who claim to give 110 percent. People who call themselves "comfortable" when what they mean is decadently rich. You're so judgmental, my shrink tells me, and I cry all the way home, thinking of it.

Later, I am talking on the phone to my sister. I walk outside with the baby on my shoulders. She reaches out, puts something in her mouth, and chokes on it. "Hold her upside down!" my sister yells. "Whack her hard on the back!" And I do until the leaf, green, still beautiful, comes out in my hand.

I develop an abiding interest in emergency precautions. I try to enlist my husband's help in this. I ask him to carry a pocketknife and a small flashlight in his backpack. Ideally, I'd like him to have one of those smoke hoods that doubles as a parachute. (If you are rich and scared enough you can buy one of these, I have read.) He thinks I have a morbid imagination. Nothing's going to happen, he says. But I want him to make promises. I want him to promise that if something happens he won't try to save people, that he'll just get home as fast as he can. He looks shaken by this request, but still I monster on about it. *Leave behind the office girl and the old lady and the fat man wheezing on the stairs.* Come home, I tell him. Save her.

A few days later the baby sees the garden hose come on and we hear her laughing.

All my life now appears to be one happy moment.
This is what the first man in space said.

Later, when it's time to go to bed, she puts both legs in one side of her footy pajamas and slyly waits for us to notice.

There is a picture of my mother holding me as a baby, a look of naked love on her face. For years, it embarrassed me. Now there is a picture of me with my daughter looking exactly the same way.

We dance with the baby every night now, spinning her round and round the kitchen. Dizzying, this happiness.

She becomes obsessed with balls. She can spot a ball-shaped object at one hundred paces. *Ball*, she calls the moon. *Ball. Ball.* On nights when it is obscured by clouds, she points angrily at the darkness.

My husband gets a new job, scoring sound tracks for commercials. The pay is better.

It has benefits. How is it, people ask. "Not bad," he says with a shrug. "Only vaguely soul-crushing."

She learns to walk. We decide to have a party to show off how persony she has become. For days beforehand, she asks me over and over, "Party now? Party now?" On the night of the festivities, I pull her wispy hair up into a ponytail. "She looks like a girl," my husband says. He seems amazed. An hour later, the guests stream in. She weaves her way in and out of them for five minutes, then tugs on my sleeve. "No more party!" she says. "Party done! Party done!"

Her favorite book is about firemen. When she sees the picture, she will mime ringing the bell and sliding down the pole. *Clang, clang, clang goes the fire engine bell. The men are on their way!*

My husband reads the book to her every night, including very very slowly the entire copyright page.

Sometimes she plays a game now where she scatters her stuffed animals all over the living room. "Babies, babies," she mutters darkly as she covers them with white napkins. "Civil War Battlefield," we call it.

One day she runs down the block by herself. I am terrified she'll forget to stop at the end. "Stop!" I scream at her. "Stop! Stop!"

"Just keep her alive until she's eighteen," my sister says. My sister has two daredevil boys, fraternal twins. She lives in the country but is always threatening to move to England. Her husband is British. He would like to solve all their problems with boarding school and compulsory backgammon. He has never liked it here. Weak-minded, he calls Americans. To make him happy, my sister serves boiled meat for dinner and makes the peas mushy.

10

Some punk rock kids move into the apartment above us. Our landlord lives in Florida so he asks us to keep an eye on them. My husband helps them carry up their three pieces of furniture and giant stereo system. I like them right away; they remind me of my students—smart, jittery, oddly earnest. "That's cool, you guys are married," the girl tells me one day, and the boy nods too as if he means it.

I have a chunk of vomit in my hair, I realize right before class. *Chunk* is maybe overstating it, but yes, something. I wash my hair in the sink. I am teaching a class called "Magic and Dread."

Sometimes I find myself having little conversations in my head with the punk rock kids upstairs.

You know what's punk rock about marriage?

Nothing.

You know what's punk rock about marriage?

All the puke and shit and piss.

My husband comes into the bathroom, holding a hammer. He is talking, reciting a litany of household things. "I fixed the wobbly chair," he tells me. "And I put a mat under the rug so that it won't ride up again. The toilet needs a new washer though. It won't stop running." This is another way in which he is an admirable person. If he notices something is broken, he will try to fix it. He won't just think about how unbearable it is that things keep breaking, that you can never fucking outrun entropy.

People keep telling me to do yoga. I tried it once at the place down the street. The only part I liked was the part at the end when the teacher covered you with a blanket and you got to pretend you were dead for ten minutes.

"Where is that second novel?" the head of my department asks me. "Tick tock. Tick tock."

We used to call her *Little. Little, come here,* we'd say. *Little, unhand the cat,* but then one day she won't let us. "I am big," she says and her face is stormy.

My old boss calls me to ask if I am looking for work. A rich man he knows needs someone to ghostwrite his book about the history of the space program. "The job pays well," he says, "but the guy's a total dick." I tell my husband about it. Yes, yes, yes, he says. It turns out we're running low on money for diapers and beer and potato chips.

What Fitzgerald said: *Once the phial was full—here is the bottle it came in. Hold on, there's a drop left there . . . No, it was just the way the light fell.*

So I meet with the rich man. It's a spectacularly ill-conceived project. He wishes to talk first about the making of the space program, then about the space race, then in the middle tell his own aggrieved story of almost but not quite making it into orbit. He'll end the book with a proposal for how we might colonize the universe, complete with elaborate technical documents of his own devising. "Sounds good," I say. "People like space." The almost astronaut is pleased. He gives me a check. "It's going to be a big book," he says. "Big!"

Sometimes at night I conduct interviews with myself.

What do you want?
I don't know.

What do you want?
I don't know.

What seems to be the problem?
Just leave me alone.

A boy who is pure of heart comes over for dinner. One of the women who is dabbling with being young again brings him. He holds himself stiffly and permits himself only the smallest of smiles at our jokes. He is ten years younger than we are, alert to any sign of compromise or dead-ending within us. "You are not allowed to compare your imagined accomplishments to our actual ones," someone says after the boy who is pure of heart leaves.

Do not jump off a wall. Do not run in the street. Do not strike your head with a stone just to see what this will do.

Of course it is difficult. You are creating a creature with a soul, my friend says.

In 1897, a French doctor named Hippolyte Baraduc conducted a series of photographic experiments. He hoped to prove that the soul does indeed reside in the body and leaves it at the moment of death. He fastened a live pigeon to a board with its wings outstretched, then placed a photographic plate on its chest and secured it tightly. As he'd hoped, when he cut the pigeon's throat the plate depicted something. The soul leaving took the form of curling eddies, he said.

Up until the seventeenth century, it was widely believed that magnets had souls. How else could an object attract or repel?

One day I see the dog-walking man kicking a mattress on the street. He kicks and kicks it. BUGS, NO GOOD, VERY BAD someone had written on it in red paint.

Baraduc claimed to be able to photograph emotions. "Hate, joy, grief, fear, sympathy, piety, & etc. No new chemical is necessary to obtain these results. Any ordinary camera will do it." He sought out emotionally agitated people, then held light-proof paper a few inches from their heads. He found that the same emotion would make the same kind of impression upon the photographic plate, but that different emotions produced different images. Anger looked like fireworks. Love was an indistinct blur.

11

There are always other mothers at the school. Some of them arrive early, and because of this it is the same ones who notice every day if I am late. These are the same mothers, the early ones, who are also good at remembering what to bring on a given day. You might have to bring a picture of your child and her father, or suntan lotion, or an empty egg carton which is to be transformed into something. Because there are mothers like me who are sometimes late to school, the teachers have built a grace period into each day. There is choice time at the beginning of the morning and if this is missed by your child it is bad, of course, but not terrible. It is not like missing circle time, where they talk about how a flower grows and what it needs (water, sun) or how we humans too are animals or how the planets are particularly arranged nearest to and farthest from the sun. All of the children know that Pluto has been demoted and they shriek with glee if their older, slower parents forget this. There is also a grace period when it comes to the bringing in of things. The day the egg carton is due is not the real day but the day before it is really really necessary, before it is really really a catastrophe not to have it. And then, even then, some teachers make provisions for the moms who forget. They may bring extra cartons or receive extras from some of the other mothers, the rememberers, the ones who are always early.

There is a story about a prisoner at Alcatraz who spent his nights in solitary confinement dropping a button on the floor then trying to find it again in the dark. Each night, in this manner, he passed the hours until dawn. I do not have a button. In all other respects, my nights are the same.

Personality Questionnaire

1. I enjoy the sensation of speeding in a car.
2. Others know me by the long hours I keep.
3. I am drawn to games of chance.

4. *Parties make me nervous.*
5. *I eat more quickly than other people.*
6. *Friends have called me thin-skinned.*
7. *I prefer indoor activities.*
8. *Often, I fear I am not up to life's challenges.*
9. *I would like to learn to fly an airplane.*
10. *Sometimes I am restless for no apparent reason.*

There is still such crookedness in my heart. I had thought loving two people so much would straighten it.

What the Yoga People say: *None of this is banal, if only you would attend to it.*

All right then, this thing clogging the sink. I reach my hand into the murky water, fiddle with the drain. When I pull it back out, my hand is scummed with grease.

My husband clears the table. Bits of meat cling to the plates, a soggy napkin floats in gravy. *In India, they say, there are men who eat only air.*

Someone has given my daughter a doctor's kit. Carefully, she takes her own temperature, places the pressure cuff around her arm. Then she takes the cuff off and examines it. "Would you like to be a doctor when you grow up?" I ask her. She looks at me oddly. "I'm already a doctor," she says.

I would give it up for her, everything, the hours alone, the radiant book, the postage stamp in my likeness, but only if she would consent to lie quietly with me until she is eighteen. If she would lie quietly with me, if I could bury my face in her hair, yes, then yes, uncle.

Student Evaluations

She is a good teacher but VERY anecdotal.
No one would call her organized.
She seems to care about her students.
She acts as if writing has no rules.

"Where is the funny?" my husband says, clicking the remote. "Bring me the funny."

What Keats said: *No such thing as the world becoming an easy place to save your soul in.*

Our beautiful Italian babysitter tells me she broke up with her boyfriend. I know him, a serious young musician who adored her. "What did he do?" I say. She makes herself a cup of tea. "He cried like a clown."

When my daughter comes home, her fingers are indelibly red and black. "Look at your hands! What happened to them?" my husband says. She looks at her hands. "I guess it is my responsibility," she tells him.

"Were the parties always so dull?" I ask my husband as we stand at the bank machine, getting money for the babysitter. He puts the bills into his wallet. "That was a $200 party," he tells me.

The Buddhists say that wisdom may be attained by reaching the three marks. The first is an understanding of the absence of self. The second is an understanding of the impermanence of all things. The third is an understanding of the unsatisfactory nature of ordinary experience.

"Everything that has eyes will cease to see," says the man on the television. He looks credentialed. His hair has a dark gleam to it. His voice is like the voices of those people who hand out flyers on the subway, but he's not talking about God or the government.

"When is everyone coming?" my daughter says. "Isn't everyone coming?" She drags her dollhouse out of her room and begins arranging and rearranging the chairs inside it. It is hard to make them as they should be, it seems. One is always askew. She is so solemn, my little girl. So solemn and precise. Carefully, she places the tiny turkey in the center of the tiny table. It is golden brown. Someone has carved a perfect flap in it. Why? I wonder. Why must everything have already begun? "Hurry," she murmurs as she works. "Hurry, hurry!"

The credentialed man is talking about the heavens now, about their most ruinous movements. The time lapse shows a field of plants perishing, a mother and child blown away by a wave of red light. Something distant and imperfectly understood is to blame for this. But the odds against it are encouraging. Astronomical even.

Still, I won't be happy until I know the name of this thing.

12

Advice for wives circa 1896: *The indiscriminate reading of novels is one of the most injurious habits to which a married woman can be subject. Besides the false views of human nature it will impart . . . it produces an indifference to the performance of domestic duties, and contempt for ordinary realities.*

It's true that I am feebleminded at the grocery store. I write lists that I forget, buy things we don't need or already have. Later, my husband will say, *did you get toilet paper, did you get ketchup, did you get garlic*, and I will say, *no, no, I forgot, sorry, here is some butterscotch pudding and some toothpicks and some whiskey sour mix*. But for now my daughter and I stand shivering in front of the meat case. "I'm cold," she says. "Why can't we go? Why do we have to stand here?" There is some kind of meat I am supposed to buy. A kind of meat to go in a meat recipe. "We can go soon," I say. "Just wait. Let me think for a minute. You're not letting me think."

So lately I've been having this recurring dream: In it, my husband breaks up with me at a party, saying, *I'll tell you later. Don't pester me.* But when I tell him this, he grows peevish. "We're married, remember? Nobody's breaking up with anybody."

"I love autumn," she says. "Look at the beautiful autumn leaves. It feels like autumn today. Is autumn your favorite time of year?" She stops walking and tugs on my sleeve. "Mommy! You are not noticing. I am using a new word. I say autumn now instead of fall."

I run into an acquaintance on the street, someone I haven't seen in years. When I knew him, we were both young. He edited a literary magazine and I sometimes wrote for him. He had a motorcycle but married early, both of which impressed me. He is still very handsome. As we talk, I discover he has a child now too.

"I think I must have missed your second book," he says.

"No," I say. "There isn't one."

He looks uncomfortable; both of us are calculating the years or maybe only I am.

"Did something happen?" he says kindly after a moment.

"Yes," I explain.

That night, I bring up my old art monster plan. "Road not taken," my husband says.

13

I had this idea in the middle of the night that maybe I could stop working for the almost astronaut and get a job writing fortune cookies instead. I could try to write really American ones. Already, I've jotted down a few of them.

Objects create happiness.
The animals are pleased to be of use.
Your cities will shine forever.
Death will not touch you.

I send my fortunes to the philosopher. He writes back immediately. *I am interested in bankrolling you. But I only have $27 in checking.*

The next morning a man comes to look at the apartment. He brings his dog with him. "Seek!" he tells the dog. "Seek! Seek!" but the dog just sits there, looking at me.

A week later, I call the man back. I give him tea and cookies. "Here's what you do," he says. "Put poison on the mattress, then on the windowsills, then in the electrical sockets. Then just go to sleep in your bed."

But the kid upstairs knows all about it already. "Can I give you a little piece of advice?" he says. "Throw out everything you own."

I read an article written by a woman living alone who got them. She talks about how depressing it is to have no one to help her with all the spraying and washing and cooking and bagging. She's spent all her money, hasn't had a date in years. I show it to my husband. "It's true. We're lucky," he says.

A few weeks later, they send a note home from her school about lice. Mothers drive across town to the Orthodox neighborhood to see the nitpicker. $100 a head is what she charges them. She is very thorough, the mothers claim. Worth every penny.

But my husband is thorough too. He goes through our hair, then holds the comb up carefully to the light.

"Do you know why I love you?" my daughter asks me. She is floating in the bathwater, her head lathered white. "Why?" I say. "Because I am your mother," she tells me.

There is a video I have seen, which I cannot unsee, that shows them avoiding the poison by climbing the far wall, crossing the ceiling, and then dropping onto the bed. And another one, even worse, in which a woman films herself waiting up all night beside her daughter's bed with a lint roller.

What Simone Weil said: *Attention without object is a supreme form of prayer.*

The almost astronaut calls me at all hours now to talk about his project. "I think it's going to be a best seller," he tells me. "Like that guy. What's his name? Sagan?"

"Carl?"

"No," he says. "That's not it. Something else. It'll come to me."

A few nights later, I secretly hope that I might be a genius. Why else can no amount of sleeping pills fell my brain? But in the morning my daughter asks me what a cloud is and I cannot say.

14

My husband listens on his headphones to a series of lectures called "The Long Now." For a long time, I hear this name without inquiring further. It seems to me a useful but imprecise phrase along the lines of "The Human Condition" or "The Life of the Mind." I am startled to learn it is in fact an organization which seeks to right the wrongs of the world. A brief survey of their website turns up lectures on topics such as Climate Change and Peak Oil. Somehow I had assumed it meant the feeling of daily life.

I find a cheap piano and surprise my husband with it. Sometimes he composes songs for us after dinner. Beautiful little things. If it is after eight, the neighbors complain. Anyway, the bugs get in it.

An Arabic proverb: *One insect is enough to fell a country.*

A Japanese proverb: *Even an insect one-tenth of an inch long has five-tenths of a soul.*

My daughter has a habit now of rifling through our drawers to see if anything inside might be of use to her. One day she unearthed the bride and groom that stood atop our wedding cake. The groom was discarded but the bride has been placed on a shelf in her room among the plastic pink horses with girlishly long manes. This is a high compliment, I discern, though my daughter does not say so explicitly.

The little jokes of the long-married. "My wife . . . She no longer believes in me," my friend says with a small wave of his hand. Everyone laughs. We are all having dinner. His wife passes me something intricate and Moroccan he has made. It is unbelievably delicious.

Are you afraid of going to the dentist?

Never Sometimes Always

I answer "sometimes" but they seem to bump me up to "always." The dentist speaks carefully to me, probing my mouth with his soft fingers. The hygienist tries to make casual conversation by asking me how many children I have. "One," I say, and she looks startled. "But you'll have another?" she asks as she rinses the blood from the sink. "No, I don't think so," I say. She shakes her head. "It just seems cruel to have an only child. I was one and it was cruel."

A Lebanese proverb: *The bedbug has a hundred children and thinks them too few.*

"Don't tell a soul," the kid warns me. "Not if you ever want anyone to visit again." He gives me some special plastic bags that zip closed tightly. At night, we can hear the bags shifting as we lie awake in bed. The deal is that if one opens up, everything in it is contaminated. Before we leave the house, we have to cook our clothes in a special cooker. Anything we are not wearing must be immediately bagged and sealed. "We're living like astronauts," my husband says, inching over to his side of the bed.

The path of a cosmonaut is not an easy, triumphant march to glory. You have to get to know the meaning not just of joy but also of grief, before being allowed in the spacecraft cabin. This is what the first man in space said.

A woman at the playground explains her dilemma. They have finally found a house, a brownstone with four floors and a garden, perfectly maintained, on the loveliest of blocks in the least anxiety producing of school districts, but now she finds that she spends much of her day on one floor looking for something that has actually been left on another floor.

I am spending hours and hours at the Laundromat now, shrinking our sweaters and unfurring her animals. One day I forget and put her blanket in. When I hand it back to her, she cries. "That was my best thing," she says. "Why would you ruin my best thing?"

15

Survival in space is a challenging endeavor. As the history of modern warfare suggests, people have generally proven themselves unable to live and work together peacefully over long periods of time. Especially in isolated or stressful situations, those living in close quarters often erupt into hostility.

Don't cook, don't fuck, what do you do? Don't cook, don't fuck, what do you do?

Einstein wondered if the moon would exist if we didn't look at it.

Russian ground control had a traditional sign-off for the cosmonauts: *May nothing be left of you, neither down nor feather.*

"What I'm looking for," the almost astronaut tells me, "is *interesting* facts."

Vladimir Komarov was the pilot on *Soyuz 1*, a spaceship that was plagued with technical problems from the start. In the weeks leading up to the launch, the cosmonaut became convinced that this would be a death mission, but the Russian politicians waved off the engineering reports. On the appointed day, a grim-faced Komarov was strapped into the spacecraft and launched into orbit. But almost immediately things began to go wrong. An antenna failed to rise. Then a solar panel malfunctioned, making the craft lopsided and difficult to navigate. Sensing a potential catastrophe, ground control aborted the mission and tried to guide Komarov home. But as he reentered the atmosphere, the spacecraft began spinning wildly. Komarov fought to control it, but it couldn't be righted.

During the long terrible descent, a politician called Komarov to tell him he was a hero. Then his wife came on the line and the couple spoke of their affairs and said good-bye. The last thing anyone heard was the cosmonaut's yells of rage and fear as his ship hurtled towards the ground. The capsule flattened instantly on impact, then burst into flames. There was no body to recover. Komarov's widow was given his charred heel bone.

But long-term survival for astronauts in space environments poses other dangers as well. Some of the most daunting challenges may, in fact, be psychological. People studying such odds look to other kinds of isolation studies for clues. The logs of polar explorers may give us the best glimpse of what it might be like to stay in space for extended periods.

Aboard the *Belgica*, off Antarctica, May 20, 1898: Explorer Frederick Cook, trapped with his men on an icebound ship, wrote the following in his log:

We are as tired of each other's company as we are of the cold monotony of the black night and of the unpalatable sameness of our food. Physically, mentally, and perhaps morally, then, we

are depressed, and from my past experience . . .
I know that this depression will increase.

"We'll get through this," I say to my husband.
"We always do." Slowly, he nods his head. I
lie on the couch in the crook of his arm. Our
clothes smell cooked.

We take turns taking her on trips. The other
one stays home, sprays the house with poison
again. Lice, she thinks they are. Neither my
husband nor I can stand to keep secrets, but
we keep this one, yes, we keep it. We learn not
to wince when people worry aloud about getting them. We hardly ever go out and if we do
we cook every bit of our clothing for hours
so as not to chance giving them to anyone.
Winter makes it harder. Before we leave the
house, we must do the scarves and mittens,
the boots and coats. When the timer goes off,
we take all the clothes out of the cooker and
then without sitting on the chair or the bed,
get dressed and leave as fast as we can.

That year we get Christmas cards from his relatives, some with those family letters tucked inside. *S got a promotion and is now a vice vice president of marketing. T has a new baby and has started an organizing business called "Sorted!" L & V have given up rice and sugar and bread.*

My husband won't let me write one. We send a smiling picture instead.

Dear Family and Friends,

It is the year of the bugs. It is the year of the pig. It is the year of losing money. It is the year of getting sick. It is the year of no book. It is the year of no music. It is the year of turning 5 and 39 and 37. It is the year of Wrong Living. That is how we will remember it if it ever passes.

With love and holiday wishes.

When we visit his parents, my daughter tries to learn to swim at the indoor pool. I watch her serious scrunched-up face, eyes closed, counting one stroke, two strokes. A few days later, she is up to fifty. Then my husband arrives from Brooklyn and she insists we rush him straight from the airport to the pool. But when we get there, she won't do it. I am tight-lipped, resentful of all the fuss she has required to be made, the great anticlimax of it. My husband falls asleep in a deck chair as we are deliberating. He has been up all night, spraying poison. His mother, bright-eyed, gentles her through the water. "Once a swimmer, always a swimmer," she says.

A thought experiment courtesy of the Stoics. If you are tired of everything you possess, imagine that you have lost all these things.

16

It is possible that I am getting too cranky and old to teach. Here I am ranting in the margins about definite vs. indefinite articles, about POV. *Think about authorial distance! Who is speaking here?*

My friend who teaches writing sometimes flips out when she is grading stories and types the same thing over and over again.

WHERE ARE WE IN TIME AND SPACE?
WHERE ARE WE IN TIME AND SPACE?

I decide to make my class read creation myths. The idea is to go back to the beginning. In some, God is portrayed as a father, in others, as a mother. When God is a father, he is said to be elsewhere. When God is a mother, she is said to be everywhere.

It's different, of course, with the art monsters. They are always elsewhere.

It was quite difficult to reach Rilke. He had no house, no address where one could find him, no steady lodging or office. He was always on his way through the world and no one, not even he himself, knew in advance which direction it would take.

This according to Stefan Zweig, one of his closest friends.

The philosopher is traveling across the country, giving lectures at colleges. He sends me his new book. It is called *Stimmung* and refers to the state of mind that precedes a schizophrenic breakdown. It is accompanied by something known as "the truth-taking stare."

Everything seems charged with meaning. "I noticed particularly" is the refrain of those who are experiencing it.

I think the philosopher is a little bit famous now. Bright-eyed girls come to his lectures and want to talk to him about how paper thin the world feels. He doesn't go out with them.

He is holding out for someone who knows how to garden.

I keep forgetting to get glasses. It makes my husband crazy. I ask my most stylish friend to come with me to pick them out. The salesman wants me to buy bright blue ones. Fashion forward, he calls them. My friend laughs. "I don't think they go with the way you dress." How do I dress? I wonder. Like a bus driver is the answer.

Three things no one has ever said about me:
You make it look so easy.
You are very mysterious.
You need to take yourself more seriously.

I get glasses that are a little bit fashion backward. *If your eyes are sound, your whole body will be filled with light.*

Just after she turns five, my daughter starts making confessions to me. It seems she is noticing her thoughts as thoughts for the first time and wants absolution. I think she must be

Catholic after all. *I thought of stepping on her foot, but I didn't. I tried to make her a little bit jealous. I pretended to be mad at him.* "Everybody has bad thoughts," I tell her. "Just try not to act on them."

At night before she goes to bed, we look at pictures of cute animals on the Internet. My husband shows me how far back the meme goes, all the way back to a big ugly cat saying: I CAN HAS CHEEZBURGER?

But my daughter is not impressed. "When can we see real animals?" she says. She wants a dog. We decide that for her birthday she can have a cat. Better for the city, my husband says. Why make a dog miserable?

Sometimes she will come in complaining about seeing things when she closes her eyes at night. Streaks of light, she says. Stars.

My husband has taken to calling me Bizarro Wife. Because when he decided not to drink anymore I talked him out of it. Because I said once that he looked sexy smoking. Because I'll give him a blow job anytime he wants, but mostly am too tired for sex. Also because I'm always saying he could quit his job if he wanted and we'll go somewhere cheap and live on rice and beans with our kid.

My husband doesn't believe me about that last bit. And why should he? Once I spent $13 on a piece of cheese. I often read catalogs meant for the rich.

But lately I'm like a beatnik in a movie. *Fuck this bourgeois shit, baby! Let's be pure of heart again!*

I have lunch with a friend I haven't seen in years. She orders things I've never heard of, sends back a piece of middling fish. I tell her various schemes to redeem my life. "I'm so compromised," she says.

17

I'm spending a lot of time online trying to buy a deserted ramshackle bungalow colony. As soon as I find one (and the money to buy it), I'm going to get ten friends to stay up there with us all summer. Kind of a commune minus the hallucinogenic drugs and the mate swapping. My husband is unmoved by my scheme. "I don't see how it will really affect me," he says. "I still have to go to work every day."

We find another apartment finally. The packing is epic, orchestrated for weeks and weeks. On the last day, the philosopher comes over and helps us drag the piano out onto the street. We put a sign on it. DON'T TAKE.

In the elevator of the new building, my daughter pushes the button for the eleventh floor. "If there were a fire, we'd have to take the stairs," I say. "But what if there were a flood?" There won't be, I tell her, not lying. For once, not.

Sometimes on the subway platform I still sway, imagining her in my arms.

Hush little baby, don't you cry, Mama's gonna sing you a lullaby, and if that mockingbird don't sing, Papa's gonna buy you a diamond ring. Mama, Dada, uh-oh, ball. Good night tree, good night stars, good night moon, good night nobody. Potato stamps, paper chains, invisible ink, a cake shaped like a flower, a cake shaped like a horse, a cake shaped like a cake, inside voice, outside voice. If you see a bad dog, stand still as a tree. Conch shells, sea glass, high tide, undertow, ice cream, fireworks, watermelon seeds, swallowed gum, gum trees, shoes and ships and sealing wax, cabbages and kings, double dares, alphabet soup, A my name is Alice and my boyfriend's name is Andy, we come from Alabama and we like apples, A my name is Alice and I want to play the game of looooove. Lightning bugs, falling stars, sea horses, goldfish, gerbils

eat their young, please, no peanut butter, paren-
tal signature required, #1 Mom, show-and-tell,
truth or dare, hide-and-seek, red light, green
light, please put your own mask on before assist-
ing, ashes, ashes, we all fall down, how to keep
the home fires burning, date night, family night,
night-night, May came home with a smooth
round stone as small as the world and as big as
alone. Stop, Drop, Roll. Salutations, Wilbur's
heart brimmed with happiness. Paper valen-
tines, rubber cement, please be mine, chicken 100
ways, the sky is falling. Monopoly, Monopoly,
Monopoly, you be the thimble, Mama, I'll be the
car.

As we're walking home from the grocery store, the plastic bags I am carrying, three to a hand, twist around my wrists. I stop and try to untwist them. There is a white band on one wrist now where the blood has fled. "Mommy," she says. "I will help you. Mommy, stand still. Mommy, let me spin them!" I let her spin them.

Three questions from my daughter:

Why is there salt in the sea?
Will you die before me?
Do you know how many dogs George Washing-
ton had?

Don't know.
Yes. Please.
36.

18

My daughter breaks both her wrists jumping off of a swing. Her friend, who is five, told her to jump off it. I promise nothing will happen, she said. But why did she promise that? she wails later at the hospital.

We have been there once before, when she stuck a plastic jewel up her nose by mistake. I tried to get it out with tweezers while my husband talked me through it on the phone, but it just went farther in. He took a cab from the city to meet us there. On the way to the hospital, she sobbed and sobbed. "Has anyone ever done this before? Has any kid ever done something like this before? Ever?" At the emergency room, we perched ridiculously on the edge of our seats, waiting for our name to be called. Hours passed. Jewel up nose = lowest mark on the triage scale.

Later my husband said, "I should have remembered this. You are only supposed to do that if you can remain very calm. Were you very calm?"

This time she is sobbing so hysterically that they can't get the X-ray for her wrists. The technician does my left hand to show her what it is. He holds the film up to the light and we all look at it. Here is the bone, shot through with emptiness, the solid ring, the haze of flesh. I think of a boy I met once on a bus who told me he was a Christian Scientist. He said they believed in idealism, which means that only the soul is real. He said once he fell off a jungle gym at school and they thought he had broken his foot, but in truth he had not broken any bones and had no pain as there were no such things as bones and pain, but only mind that could feel nothing. I remember that I wanted to be a Christian Scientist then. But in time this passed.

Afterwards, incredibly, they give her morphine. She begins to talk dreamily about doughnuts. How she will get a dozen as a reward for this and take one bite out of each of them.

We take our daughter to the doctor's office to get the casts. After he puts them on, he warns her not to drop anything in them. "If you do, you will have to come back and have them removed, then put on again under anesthesia," he says. We leave the office.

Something fell into my cast.

What?

I don't know.

But you're sure something did?

No, maybe. Maybe I just thought it.

You just thought it?

No, I felt it.

You felt it?

Maybe.

What was it?

I don't know. Something.

What?

Nothing, I think. Maybe something.

What?

Nothing. No, something.

We wash her hair in a bucket, try to scratch her wrists with a chopstick. It is summer and she cries because she wants to swim.

What Wittgenstein said: *What you say, you say in a body; you can say nothing outside of this body.*

One night we let her sleep in our room because the air conditioner is better. We all pile into the big bed. There is a musty animal smell to her casts now. She brings in the night-light that makes fake stars and places it on the bedside table. Soon everyone is asleep but me. I lie in our bed and listen to the hum of the air conditioner and the soft sound of their breathing. Amazing. Out of dark waters, this.

19

On our seventh anniversary, my husband plays a song for me, but it's almost too sad to hear. It's about marriage and who will go first. *One of us will die inside these arms* is the chorus.

Hard to believe I used to think love was such a fragile business. Once when he was still young, I saw a bit of his scalp showing through his hair and I was afraid. But it was just a cowlick. Now sometimes it shows through for real, but I feel only tenderness.

He misses his piano, I think. But he doesn't talk about it. I give him a recording of Edison explaining his phonograph.

Your words are preserved in tinfoil and will come back upon the application of the instrument years after you are dead in exactly the same tone of voice you spoke them in . . . This tongueless, toothless instrument, without larynx or pharynx, dumb voiceless matter, nevertheless mimics your tones, speaks with your voice, utters your words, and centuries after you have crumbled into dust will repeat again and again, to a generation that could never know you, every idle thought, every fond fancy, every vain word that you chose to whisper against this iron diaphragm.

Our words are preserved in tinfoil and will come back upon the application of this instrument and so we try as much as we can to speak kindly to each other.

When we met, he wore glasses he'd had for fifteen years. I had the same bangs I did in college. I used to plot to break those glasses secretly, but I never told him how much I hated them until the day he came home with new ones.

I think it was a year later that I grew out my bangs. When they were finally gone, he said, "I've always hated bangs actually."

My sister shakes her head at this story. "You have a kid-glove marriage," she says.

She's moving to England. That bastard husband of hers.

20

The almost astronaut has become obsessed with *Voyager 1* and *Voyager 2* and the Golden Record. He'd like me to put everything that's ever been written about them into his manuscript. I tell him I think the story is too well-known, that we should look for something less expected. But he shakes his head. "Give the people what they want. That's the first rule of business." He made his fortune selling bug zappers. Last year, I got one as a Christmas present. I ask him what the second rule of business is. "Always be efficient," he says.

I think about this rule. What would my life be like if I followed it? It is true that the almost astronaut never wastes a minute. There are always energy bar wrappers in the bathroom trash can. He eats while on the toilet.

That night, my daughter asks me to read to her from a book her teacher has given her.

In it, alliteratively named animals go on extremely modest adventures and return with lessons learned. A child in a wheelchair is thoughtfully penciled in in the background. My daughter yawns as I finish it. "Tell me a better story," she says.

I tell her about *Voyager 1* and *2* and the Golden Record. They were like messages in a bottle, I explain, but thrown into outer space instead of the ocean. My daughter is mildly interested. She wants to know what sounds were recorded for the aliens. I find the list and read it to her.

Music of the Spheres
Volcanoes, Earthquake, Thunder
Mud Pots
Wind, Rain, Surf
Crickets, Frogs
Birds, Hyena, Elephant
Whale Song
Chimpanzee
Wild Dog

Footsteps, Heartbeat, Laughter
The First Tools
Tame Dog
Herding Sheep, Birdsong, Blacksmith, Sawing
Riveter
Morse Code, A Ship's Horn
Horse and Cart
Train
Tractor, Bus, Auto
F-111 Flyby, Saturn 5 *Liftoff*
Kiss, Mother and Child
Life Signs, Pulsar

My husband is hunched over his computer, just as he was when I went in. All day long he has been following the news about an earthquake in another country. Every time the death count is updated, he updates me. I open the window. The air is cold, but it smells sweet. Outside, someone is yelling something about something. *Give the people what they want,* I think.

A few weeks later, the almost astronaut calls me to tell me that *Voyager 2* may be nearing the edge of our galaxy. "Perfect timing," he says. "We'll tie it into marketing."

I tell him I have too much work to do already, but he insists that we move quickly. "I'll pay you more," he says. "Much more." He even hires an intern to fact-check for me.

I have an intern. All of my life now appears to be one happy moment.

It turns out there is a famous love story attached to the Golden Record project. A "cosmic" love story is how I describe it to the intern because who can resist the urge to say silly things about Carl Sagan? *If you wish to make an apple pie from scratch, you must first invent the Universe.* I remember how he stood there in that turtleneck, an oven mitt on his hand.

I fill him in on how the project started in 1976 when NASA asked Sagan to assemble a committee to decide what exactly this celestial mix tape should contain. It took almost two years to decide everything. Carl Sagan and his wife, Linda, collaborated on the project. They even enlisted their six-year-old son to do one of the greetings. Other key members of the team included the astronomer Frank Drake and the writers Ann Druyan and Timothy Ferris. The engineers constructed the record so that it might survive for a billion years.

The Golden Record included greetings in fifty-four human and one whale language, ninety minutes of music from around the world, and 117 pictures of life on Earth. These pictures were meant to suggest the widest possible range of human experiences. Only two things were off-limits. NASA decreed that no pictures could depict sex and no pictures could depict violence. No sex because NASA was prudish and no violence because images of ruins or bombs exploding might be interpreted by aliens as threatening. Ann Druyan tells what happened next.

In the course of my daunting search for the single most worthy piece of Chinese music, I phoned

Carl and left a message at his hotel in Tucson . . . An hour later the phone rang in my apartment in Manhattan. I picked it up and heard a voice say: "I got back to my room and found a message that said Annie called. And I asked myself, why didn't you leave me that message ten years ago?"

Bluffing, joking, I responded lightheartedly. "Well, I've been meaning to talk to you about that, Carl." And then, more soberly, "Do you mean for keeps?"

"Yes, for keeps," he said tenderly. "Let's get married."

"Yes," I said, and that moment we felt we knew what it must be like to discover a new law of nature.

So there it is, the famous cosmic love story. But like most love stories there turns out to be more to it. *This timeline doesn't make sense,* the intern writes in the margin. *Isn't Sagan already married?*

That night, my husband complains that I'm working too much. He grumbles about the overflowing trash and the out-of-season fruit rotting in the fridge. I clean out all the moldy things and empty all the trash cans. I line the garbage bags up by the door before I take them out, hoping he will comment. He gives me a look. The one that means: *What do you want? A medal?*

The kiss was the trickiest sound to capture, the engineers said. Some of the ones they tried were too loud, others too quiet. *In the end, the kiss that landed on the record was one that Timothy Ferris planted on his fiancée Ann Druyan's cheek.* The intern takes his yellow marker and highlights this for me.

The blip in that cosmic love story then. Ann Druyan was engaged to marry Timothy Ferris while they were working on the *Voyager* project with Carl Sagan and his wife, Linda. Then Carl and Ann decided to get married. The news took a while to reach Linda and Timothy. Or so my intern says. But when Ann Druyan tells the story, that part is missing, like a record that skips.

She talks instead about how she went into a laboratory just two days after that phone call. She was hooked up to a computer and began to meditate. All the data from her brain and heart was turned into sound for the Golden Record.

To the best of my abilities I tried to think about the history of ideas and human social organization. I thought about the predicament that our civilization finds itself in and about the violence and poverty that make this planet a hell for so many of its inhabitants. Toward the end I permitted myself a personal statement of what it was like to fall in love.

According to *People* magazine, Carl and Linda Sagan's divorce was "acrimonious."

21

The Yoga People always travel in pairs, their mats under their arms, their hair severely shorn in that new mother way. But what if someone sucker punched them and took their mats away? How long until they'd knuckle under?

Would you like to run the fun fair? Would you like to join the compost committee? Would you like to organize the coat drive? Would you like to teach a puppetry elective?

A student asked Donald Barthelme how he might become a better writer. Barthelme advised him to read through the whole history of philosophy from the pre-Socratics up through the modern-day thinkers. The student wondered how he could possibly do this. "You're probably wasting time on things like eating and sleeping," Barthelme said. "Cease that, and read all of philosophy and all of literature." Also art, he amended. Also politics.

There are 60 seconds in a minute, 60 minutes in an hour, 24 hours in a day, 7 days in a week, 52 weeks in a year, and X years in a life. Solve for X.

What T. S. Eliot said: *When all is said and done the writer may realize that he has wasted his youth and wrecked his health for nothing.*

She will not go to college if that means she must go away from me. When she has a baby, she will come and stay with me for a month and I will help her care for the baby and then she will go away for one day, then she will come back again and stay for a month or a year. She does not ever want to live away from me, she explains. "Promise?" I say. She curls up in my arms, all elbows and knees. "Promise."

My Very Educated Mother Just Serves Us Noodles. This is the mnemonic they give her to remember the order of the planets.

Once when she was just learning to talk, I ran my hand across her face, naming every part of it. Later, when I put her in the crib, she called me back. First, she asked for water, then for milk, then for kisses. "It hurts. Don't go," she said. "What does? What hurts, sweetie?" She paused. "My eyelashes."

Some women make it look so easy, the way they cast ambition off like an expensive coat that no longer fits.

Stop writing I love you, said the note my daughter wrote over the one I left in her lunchbox. For a long time, she had asked for a note like that every day, but now a week after turning six, she puts a stop to it. I feel odd, strangely light-headed when I read the note. It is a feeling from a long time ago, the feeling of someone breaking up with me suddenly. My husband kisses me. "Don't worry, love. Really, it's nothing."

There is a husband who requires mileage receipts, another who wants sex at three a.m. One who forbids short haircuts, another who refuses to feed the pets. I would never put up with that, all the other wives think. Never.

But my agent has a theory. She says every marriage is jerry-rigged. Even the ones that look reasonable from the outside are held together inside with chewing gum and wire and string.

So now this woman at the playground is telling me about how her husband rifles through her purse for receipts. If he finds one for the wrong kind of ATM, he posts it on the refrigerator, highlighted in red. She shrugs. "He can't help it."

What exactly am I waiting for her to say? That she married a fool? That her house is built on ashes? And here I am, the lucky one for once. Such blinding good fortune to have married him.

The wives have requirements too, of course. What they require is this: *unswerving obedience. Loyalty unto death.*

My husband sits in our kitchen and hand-sews a book. I hope that when it goes through the post office no machine will touch it.

22

How Are You?

soscaredsoscaredsoscaredsoscaredsoscared
soscaredsoscaredsoscaredsoscaredsoscared
soscaredsoscaredsoscaredsoscaredsoscared
soscaredsoscaredsoscaredsoscaredsoscared
soscaredsoscaredsoscaredsoscaredsoscared
soscaredsoscaredsoscaredsoscaredsoscared
soscaredsoscaredsoscaredsoscaredsoscared
soscaredsoscaredsoscaredsoscaredsoscared
soscaredsoscaredsoscaredsoscaredsoscared
soscaredsoscaredsoscaredsoscaredsoscared
soscaredsoscaredsoscaredsoscaredsoscared
soscaredsoscaredsoscaredsoscaredsoscared
soscaredsoscaredsoscaredsoscaredsoscared
soscaredsoscaredsoscaredsoscaredsoscared
soscaredsoscaredsoscaredsoscaredsoscared
soscaredsoscaredsoscaredsoscaredsoscared
soscaredsoscaredsoscaredsoscaredsoscared
soscaredsoscaredsoscaredsoscaredsoscared

The wife is praying a little. To Rilke, she thinks.

It is important if someone asks you to remember one of your happiest times to consider not only the question but also the questioner. If the question is asked by someone you love, it is fair to assume that this person hopes to feature in this recollection he has called forth. But you could, if you were wrong and if you had a crooked heart, forget this most obvious and endearing thing and instead speak of a time you were all alone, in the country, with no one wanting a thing from you, not even love. You could say that was your happiest time. And if you did this then telling about this happiest of times would cause the person you most want to be happy to be unhappy.

In the year 134 B.C., Hipparchus observed a new star. Until that moment he had believed steadfastly in the permanence of them. He then set out to catalog all the principal stars so as to know if any others appeared or disappeared.

They were in the coffee shop that day he asked her. *When were you the happiest?* Something she should have seen then, something about the look on his face, the way the air changed in that moment.

So how come it took her a month to think of her own question? The one he answered rhetorically.

Is that what you think this is about?

And then there is the night that he misses putting their daughter to bed. He calls to say he is leaving work right when she thinks he will be home, something he has never done before.

And so slowly, stupidly, she asks the question again.

Why would you even say that?

He falls asleep. All night, she lies there beside him, listening to him breathe. Her whole body is prickling. She feels hot then cold then hot again. *I noticed particularly,* she thinks. The minute it is light out she wakes him.

That's not what I asked you.

His eyes, god, his eyes, in the moment before he nodded his head.

Thales supposed the Earth to be flat and to float upon water.

Anaxagoras thought the moon was an inhabited Earth.

Her sister drives in from Pennsylvania at five a.m. to pick up the daughter. "Don't worry," she says. "I'll take her on an adventure. She won't know anything. Not yet at least."

What Ovid said: *If you are ever caught, no matter how well you've concealed it / Though it is as clear as the day, swear up and down it is a lie / Don't be too abject, and don't be too unduly attentive / That would establish your guilt far above anything else / Wear yourself out if you must and prove in her bed, that you could / Not / Possibly be that good, coming from some other girl.*

Taller?
Thinner?
Quieter?
Easier, he says.

In 2159 B.C., the royal astronomers Hi and Ho were executed because they failed to predict an eclipse.

23

Researchers looked at magnetic resonance images of the brains of people who described themselves as newly in love. They were shown a photograph of their beloveds while their brains were scanned for activity. The scan showed the same reward systems being activated as in the brains of addicts given a drug.

Ca-ching! Ca-ching! Ca-ching!

For most married people, the standard pattern is a decrease of passionate love, but an increase in deep attachment. It is thought that this attachment response evolved in order to keep partners together long enough to have and raise children. Most mammals don't raise their offspring together, but humans do.

There is nowhere to cry in this city. But the wife has an idea one day. There is a cemetery half a mile from their apartment. Perhaps one could wander through it sobbing without unnerving anyone. Perhaps one could flap one's hands even.

In many tribal cultures children are considered self-sufficient at or near the age of six. For all practical purposes, this means if they were lost overnight in the wild they might not perish. Of course, in modern industrial societies, children tend to be protected much longer. But there's evidence that the age six still resonates with men. Researchers say that many men have affairs around the time their oldest child turns six. Chances are their genes will still march on even without direct oversight.

Eat the black berries! Not the red! Daddy has to go away for a little while. And don't talk to the bears!

"How is that even possible?" the philosopher says. "He's one of the kindest people I've ever met."

She knows. She knows. So it begs the question, doesn't it? Did she unkind and ungood and untrue him?

24

The wife goes to yoga now. Just to shut everyone up. She goes to it in a neighborhood where she does not live and has never lived. She takes the class meant for old and sick people but can still hardly do any of it. Sometimes she just stands and looks out the window where the people whose lives are intact enough not to have to take yoga live. Sometimes the wife cries as she is twisting her body into positions. There is a lot of crying in the class for the old and sick people so no one says anything.

But even the wife notices that her teacher is arrayed in light. The teacher takes pity on her and gives her private lessons. The wife tells her about the husband. About how he may or may not love someone else. About how she may or may not leave him. She tells her that they viciously whisper-fight at night when her daughter is in bed.

She does not say, Last night, I pulled his hair. Last night I tried to pull his hair out of his head.

It is so easy now for the wife to be patient and kind to the daughter. She will never love anyone or anything more. Never. It is official.

She remembers the first night she knew she loved him, the way the fear came rushing in. She laid her head on his chest and listened to his heart. One day this too will stop, she thought. The no, no, no of it.

Why would you ruin my best thing?

Her neighbor's husband fell in love with a girl who served coffee to him every morning. She was twenty-three and wanted to be a dancer or a poet or a physical therapist. When he left his family, his wife said, "Does it matter to you how foolish you look? That all our friends find you ridiculous?" He stood in the doorway, his coat in his hand. "No," he said.

The wife watched her neighbor get fat over the next year. The Germans have a word for that. *Kummerspeck*. Literally, *grief bacon*.

Love is the word men use to paper over this.

Studies show that 110% of men who leave their wives for other women report that their wives are crazy.

Darwin theorized that there was something left over after sexual attractiveness had served its purpose and compelled us to mate. This he called "beauty" and thought it might be what drives the human animal to make art.

Every single song has a message for the wife these days. Some are particularly moving and must be played on repeat over and over as she walks to the subway. For example: *Watergate does not bother me. Does your conscience bother you? Tell me true.*

No one gets the crack-up he expects. The wife was planning for the one with the headscarf and the dark jokes and the people speaking kindly of her at her funeral.

Oh wait, might still get that one.

We both felt really bad about it, the husband tells the wife. "Oh, the hand-wringing!" her best friend says. "Do they think they're in a movie?"

Sometimes the husband and wife run into each other in the park across the street. He is there to smoke, she to stare at the trees. He buttons the three buttons of her coat. *He loves me, he loves me not, he loves me,* she thinks. Both have trouble working up the nerve to go into the Little Theater of Hurt Feelings. They joke that they should just run off to Mexico together. Forget this whole stupid thing.

But in they go. It is the designated place for questions.
   "Are you still e-mailing or calling her?"
   "No," he says.

"Are you still sending her music?"

"No," he says slowly. "I'm not sending her music."

"What? What are you sending her?"

"Just one video," he says.

"Of what?"

"Of guinea pigs eating a watermelon."

What Kant said: *What causes laughter is the sudden transformation of a tense expectation into nothing.*

What the Girl said: *Hey, I really like you.*

25

The wife thinks the old word is better. She says he is *besotted*. The shrink says he is *infatuated*. She doesn't want to tell what the husband says.

Anyway, he takes it back a few days in.

I am not very observant, the wife thinks. Once her husband bought a dining room table and it wasn't until dinnertime that she noticed it. By then he was angry.

These are the sorts of things they talk about in the Little Theater of Hurt Feelings.

But she does get irritated when her college sends around the memo at the end of the semester about how to recognize a suicidal student. She wants to send it back marked up in black letters. *How about you look in their eyes?*

People say, *You must have known. How could you not know?* To which she says, Nothing has ever surprised me more in my life.

You must have known, people say.

The wife did have theories about why he was acting gloomy. He was drinking too much, for example. But no, that turned out to be completely backwards; all the whiskey drinking was the result, not the cause, of the problem. Correlation IS NOT causation. She remembered that the almost astronaut always got very agitated about this mistake that nonscientists made.

Other theories she'd had about the husband's gloominess:

He no longer has a piano.
He no longer has a garden.
He no longer is young.

She found a community garden and a good therapist for him, then went back to talking about her own feelings and fears while he patiently listened.

Was she a good wife?
Well, no.

Evolution designed us to cry out if we are being abandoned. To make as much noise as possible so the tribe will come back for us.

The ex-boyfriend starts sending her music. Rare cuts, B-sides, little perfect things. He wants to make amends, she remembers.

She did speed with him once. But it is not the best drug for her. Her brain tends to speed along anyway, speed, swerve, crash, and so on and so on. That is the default state of things.

Some nights in bed the wife can feel herself floating up towards the ceiling. Help me, she thinks, help me, but he sleeps and sleeps.

"What is he acting like?" her best friend says. Like an Evil Love Zombie is the answer.

That first time they fucked after she found out. Jesus. Jesus. He looking down at her body which was not the girl's body, she looking up at his face which was not his face. "I'm sorry I let you get so lonely," she told him later. "Stop apologizing," he said.

What John Berryman said: *Let all flowers wither like a party.*

The wife reads about something called "the wayward fog" on the Internet. The one who has the affair becomes enveloped in it. His old life and wife become unbearably irritating. His possible new life seems a shimmering dream. All of this has to do with chemicals in the brain, allegedly. An amphetamine-like mix, far more compelling than the soothing attachment one. Or so the evolutionary biologists say.

It is during this period that people burn

their houses down. At first the flames are beautiful to see. But later when the fog wears off, they come back to find only ashes.

"What are you reading about?" the husband asks her from across the room. "Weather," she tells him.

26

People keep flirting with the wife. Has this been happening all along and she never noticed? Or is it new? She's like a taxi whose light just went on. All these men standing in the street, waving her over.

I CAN HAS BOYFRIEND?

She falls in love with a friend. She falls in love with a student. She falls in love with the bodega man. He hands her back her change so gently.

Floating, yes, floating away. How can he sleep? Doesn't he feel her levitating?

I will leave you, my love. Already I am going. Already I watch you speaking as if from a great height. Already the feel of your hand on my hand, of your lips on my lips, is only curious. It is decided then. The stars are accelerating. I half remember a sky could look like this. I saw it once when she was born. I saw it once when I got sick. I thought you'd have to die before I saw it again. I thought one of us would have to die. But look, here it is! Who will help me? Who can help me? Rilke? Rilke! If you're listening, come quickly. Lash me to this bed! Bind me to this earthly body! If you hear this, come now! I am untethering. Who can hold me?

What John Berryman said: *Goodbye, sir, & fare well. You're in the clear.*

These bits of poetry that stick to her like burrs.

Lately, the wife has been thinking about God, in whom the husband no longer believes. The wife has an idea to meet her ex-boyfriend at the park. Maybe they could talk about God. Then make out. Then talk about God again.

She tells the yoga teacher that she is trying to be honorable. *Honorable!* Such an old-fashioned word, she thinks. Ridiculous, ridiculous.

"Yes, be honorable," the yoga teacher says.

Whenever the wife wants to do drugs, she thinks about Sartre. One bad trip and then a giant lobster followed him around for the rest of his days.

Also she signed away the right to self-destruct years ago. The fine print on the birth certificate, her friend calls it.

So she invents allergies to explain her red eyes and migraines to explain the blinked-back look of pain. One day, coming out of their building, she staggers a little from the exhaustion of all of it. Her elderly neighbor comes over, touches her sleeve. "Are you okay, dear?" he asks. Carefully, politely, she shakes him off of her.

Sometimes when the wife is trying to do positions, the yoga teacher will single her out for instruction. The wife can't help but notice that she never has to correct other students in this particular way.

Do not instruct the head! The head is not being instructed!

How has she become one of those people who wears yoga pants all day? She used to make fun of those people. With their happiness maps and their gratitude journals and their bags made out of recycled tire treads. But now it seems possible that the truth about getting older is that there are fewer and fewer things to make fun of until finally there is nothing you are sure you will never be.

27

He sent the girl a love letter over the radio. Later, the wife sees his playlist from that night. It is from the night before she went out of town. The night before it first happened. She listens to the songs he played one by one, ticking each of them off the list.

Afterwards, the wife sits on the toilet for a long time because her stomach is twisting. She feels something rising in her throat and spits into her daughter's pink plastic bucket. Just a little bile. She dry-heaves again, but nothing. The longer she sits there, the more she notices how dingy and dirty the bathroom is. There is a tangle of hair on the side of the sink, some kind of creeping mildew on the shower curtain. Their towels are no longer white and are fraying along the edges. Her underwear too is dinged nearly gray. The elastic is coming out a little. Who would wear such a thing? What kind of repulsive creature? She takes her underwear off and wraps it around and around in toilet paper, then puts it in the bottom of the trash where no one will see.

When you pick up one piece of dust, the entire world comes with it.

"I am alone," her student says. "Everyone is tired of this. No one will come anymore." But Lia is only twenty-four. She is beautiful and brilliant. There are so many more years when people will come.

Your friends and students adore you.

The wife loses a twenty-dollar bill somewhere between the store and home, but she can't make herself go back to look for it. In the last store, the clerk was unkind to her or at least not kind.

I only wanted you to adore me.

28

She goes to visit Lia in a hospital in Westchester. Her wrists are bandaged but her eyes have a little light in them. "Thank you for coming," she says formally, as if she is in a receiving line at a wedding.

The wife has been teaching for twenty years. It is not the first time she's been at the bedside of someone with bandaged wrists.

She brings Lia a notebook, spiral-bound. But they won't let her take it. No wire, they say. She should have thought of that. Lia called her right before the lights went out. There's that moment, you know, for most people, where you decide you want to wake up in the world one more day.

Everyone there won't do something. There is a small flock of dull-eyed girls who hate to eat, who hide measuring spoons in their coats and leave clumps of hair in the sink, and then there are the ones who never answer questions no matter how many different ways you ask them. Sleep is the thing Lia won't do. She never sleeps unless they drug her. But she never rings the call button in the middle of the night either. "I just wait for first light," she says. "I watch the window."

This is how the wife gets through the nights too, but she doesn't tell her this.

Lia was legally dead for one minute but she said she didn't see anything, that there was only darkness and a low hum like a vacuum cleaner running.

Now the wife is sitting with her on a porch, looking at the trees. There are trees everywhere you look at this place. Someone, long ago, must have believed that trees could solve anything. The other patients take turns blowing bubbles from a small container because they are not allowed to smoke or drink here. "The great green earth," Lia calls it, but not as a joke, more like it breaks her heart to say it. "Stay," the wife tells her. "Just stay."

29

Enough already with the terrible hunted eyes of the married people. Did everyone always look this way but she is just now seeing it?

Case in point: The wife runs into C at a party, a brilliant woman married to a brilliant man. She has just had a show at a major gallery. Her husband is in the MoMA permanent collection. Brilliant, brilliant. But C does not talk to the wife about brilliant things. She talks about her dissembling contractor, about spa treatments, about waiting lists for private kindergarten. Later the husband asks, "Oh, you saw C, how was she?" "She was radiating rage," the wife says.

If only they were French, the wife thinks. This would all feel different. But no, *feel* isn't the word exactly. What is it that the grad students say?
Signify.

It would all *signify* differently.

General notes: If the wife becomes unwived, what should she be called? Will the story have to be rewritten? There is a time between being a wife and being a divorcée, but no good word for it. Maybe say what a politician might say. Stateless person. Yes, stateless.

Either way it's going to be terrible for a long time, the shrink says.

Here is what happens in middle age: Some friends and acquaintances who were merely eccentric for years become unmistakably mad. K tells the wife the story of a childhood friend who wears too much makeup now, who seems always to be sweating. This friend asked if she could come and cook a meal for K and her husband at their housewarming party. "No, no, just bring yourself," she said. "We have everything." The woman arrived at the party, sweating, carrying a bag of kale and raw meat.

The wife is afraid. She is afraid again in the old way. She'd thought it was done. Until he died. ("If he died," she almost said. "If " she loved him so much she contrived to say.) She did say "loved," she noticed.

"Tense! Tense!" the wife has always said to her students, trying to explain that it matters, that it illuminates things.

They used to send each other letters. The return address was always the same: *Dept. of Speculation.*

All of the letters are still in their house; he has a box of them on his desk, as does she.

"I just feel . . . ," she says. The shrink cuts her off. "I know, I know, everyone always knows exactly what you feel, don't they?"

"What about me?" Her daughter likes to ask this whenever the conversation veers out of her comprehension. "What about me?" A chip off the old block, the wife thinks.

The wife has taken to laughing maniacally when the husband says something, then repeating the word back incredulously.

Nice????

Fun????

She has seen this rhetorical strategy used before by a soon-to-be ex-wife talking to her soon-to-be ex-husband. Poor creature, she thought then.

30

The undergrads get the suicide jokes, but the ones about divorce go right over their heads.

You're a truth bomb, a cute guy said to her once at a party. Before excusing himself to go flirt with someone else.

Q. Why couldn't the Buddhist vacuum in corners?

A. Because she had no attachments.

The wife is advised to read a horribly titled adultery book. She takes the subway three neighborhoods away to buy it. The whole experience of reading it makes her feel compromised, and she hides it around the house with the fervor another might use to hide a gun or a kilo of heroin. In the book, he is referred to as the participating partner and she as the hurt one. There are many other icky things, but there is one thing in the book that makes her laugh out loud. It is in a footnote about the way different cultures handle repairing a marriage after an affair.

In America, the participating partner is likely to spend an average of 1,000 hours processing the incident with the hurt partner. This cannot be rushed.

When she reads this, the wife feels very very sorry for the husband.

Who is only about 515 hours in.

31

In Epirus, there is a kind of spider called "the sunless one." The Cypriots called the viper "the deaf one." The idea was to give such dangerous creatures a sort of code name, one that is calculated to leave them unaware that they have been mentioned. The fear was that to mention such a creature was to cause it to appear.

Her sister has a deal with her husband. *Whatever happens, keep it like in the fifties. Not one word ever. Make sure she's a nobody.*

Towards the end, the baby hadn't been growing quite as she should be and so once a week the doctors had the wife come in to be tested. She'd sit in a recliner, hooked up to the machines, waiting to hear the heartbeat. Each time, the wife feared she wouldn't hear it, but then there it would be, a sound like horses galloping. The way he looked at her when they heard it. It seemed impossible to feel more than they did.

Always always, he wrote in the book he gave the wife last Christmas.

The sunless one? The deaf one? The cubicled one?

The wife gets an expensive haircut. She shops for something to wear to the husband's office. She is going to meet him there for lunch; they have decided to try this. This civilized French-seeming thing. In the end, the wife buys only a pair of boots and takes them home without even trying them on. Later, she opens the box and looks at them. The heels are higher than she usually wears. They look uncomfortable. So why does she want to wear uncomfortable shoes on this the most uncomfortable of all days?

Oh, right, she thinks. Evolution.

BECAUSE I AM A BIGGER BIRD THAN YOU!

She wears her black sneakers and jeans and a shirt someone cool once said was cool.

32

She would not have let one of her students write the scene this way. Not with the pouring rain and the wife's broken umbrella and the girl in her long black coat. To begin with, she'd suggest taking out the first scene on the subway, the boring one, where the wife pretends to be a Buddhist. (I am a person, she is a person, I am a person, she is a person etc. etc.) *Needed? Can this be shown through gesture?*

She would ask for more details of the girl's appearance. She'd cut the implausible handshake and point out how stilted the dialogue is. *(You have caused my family great pain. I don't want to be an abstraction to you anymore.)* She might pencil in the girl crying or saying some small thing. *Surely she feels something? Wasn't there hand-wringing?* She'd slow down the moment before the girl turns on her heel without a word and leaves them. *Nothing else here?*

She'd point out that what's interesting is

actually the lead-up to the scene. How the wife takes a picture of herself before she leaves the house, how she looks somehow as if she is standing in a wind tunnel, how the husband calls her just as she gets off the subway and says, "Don't come here. A change of plans. I'll meet you outside." The husband says he couldn't help it; he told the girl she was stopping by. "She'll come out here instead," he says. But the girl doesn't do it. She stays and hides in the office. *Perhaps a bit more about how the wife feels?* How she feels something she's never felt before surge through her body, how she stands on a corner in Midtown at one in the afternoon, kicking a newspaper machine, screaming, "You fucked a child! She's a fucking child! Tell her to come out here!" *This is very emotionally charged,* she'd write next to the moment when the husband calls the girl and softly tries to convince her. Softly saying, just come, please, so tender his voice, so sorry to cause the girl pain, and all because of the scene his crazy wife is making, his wife yelling in the background. Yelling and yelling.

Then the wife stops yelling and says slowly and clearly to the husband, "Tell her if she doesn't come, I'll come to her job, and if she quits this job, I'll come to her apartment and if she leaves that apartment, I'll come to her new one. Tell her I'll find her. Tell her I'm great at research. Tell her I'm fucking great at it. I'll fucking find her one way or another." People avert their eyes as they pass. "Just come out," he says. "Please? Please? It's going to happen sometime."

It is raining harder now. They are getting drenched. "Ten minutes!" the wife screams in the background. "Ten fucking minutes! That's all I want!" His wife who has hardly ever yelled at him and never in public. *It's important to note the POV switch here.* The wife notices that her foot hurts from kicking the newspaper machine. She wonders if she's broken it. *Add a pause here. A little beat before the action continues.* The husband hangs up the phone. His hands are shaking. "She's coming," he says. "She'll be here in a bit."

But it's a long time still. They stand on the

designated corner. There is, of course, the theatrical rain. The wife knows which direction the girl will be coming from and she thinks that she should stand back in the doorway, that it would be kinder that way, because it will be hard for this girl to walk towards her. So she lets her husband stand out there in the street and then when she knows the girl has come from the look on his face she steps out and greets her in the rain. The girl is shorter than she expected. Long red hair. Glasses, fashion-forward ones. She stands there shaking. With fear, the wife thinks. Or no, something else maybe. The girl stands there rigidly as the wife speaks. Then the moment the words stop she turns and walks away.

The husband and wife walk in the other direction. It is a block before they speak. "She has pretty eyes," the wife says. They walk towards a bar, prearranged. He holds the door open for her. "Wait, did she have bangs?"

33

"Haven't you punished us enough?" the husband says a few days later. *Us?* the wife thinks. *Did he say us? Holy shit.*

She learns something new, something that sends a chill through her. The girl made him go for a walk with her the next day. Correction—he went on a walk with the girl the next day.

The husband doesn't volunteer this. Like every detail it is eked out of him in the Little Theater of Hurt Feelings. "She was furious," he explains. "She felt ambushed."

Sorry, the wife thinks of saying. *Sorry, sorry.*

But that night, in the taxi, she does not concern herself with his voice, which is low and grievous, but only with the position of the moon in the sky. How she can make it disappear with one small movement of her thumb.

Hahahahahahayoustupidcunthahahahahaha

"Am I winking?" the daughter asks them when they get home. One of her eyes is closed, the other twitching.

"Not quite," he says.

"Now? Now?"

Two Jokes

1. A man is standing on the bank of a river when it suddenly begins to flood. His wife and his mistress are both being swept away. Who should he save?

His wife. (Because his mistress will always understand.)

2. A man is standing on the bank of a river when it suddenly begins to flood. His wife and his mistress are both being swept away. Who should he save?

His mistress. (Because his wife will never understand.)

34

The wife is reading *Civilization and Its Discontents*, but she keeps getting lost in the index.

Analogies
   bare leg on a cold night, 40
   cautious businessman, 34
   guest who becomes a permanent lodger, 53
   Polar expedition, ill equipped, 98

When she tells people she might move to the country, they say, "But aren't you afraid you're going to get lonely?"
   Get?

Imaging studies have found that the pain involved in romantic breakups is not just emotional. Similar areas to the ones that process physical assault light up in the brains of the recently jilted.

What John Berryman said: *I'm too alone. I see no end. If we could all run, even that would be better.*

At night, they lie in bed holding hands. It is possible if she is stealthy enough that the wife can do this while secretly giving the husband the finger.

Grow old with me. The best is yet to be, say the cards in the anniversary section.

But there are other lines from Yeats the wife keeps remembering.

Consume my heart away; sick with desire
And fastened to a dying animal

Things fall apart.

"The girl had red hair," the wife tells her sister. "The same color I used to dye mine."

The wife stopped dyeing her hair when she got pregnant. (Because of the monster babies with no hands that the vain hair-dyeing women have.) But she never went back to it and for years now her hair has been streaked with gray.

Spell for invocation of divorce: *Greener!*
Greener!

Sometimes she talks to the husband in her
head. *You think I don't know. I know. Once I*
was sleeping next to that boy and a mouse ran
through my hair, but I didn't move. I didn't want
to risk him getting out of bed.

The only love that feels like love is the doomed
kind. (Fun fact.)

I was hoping your happiest memory might in-
clude me.

Later the wife realizes what that was, why he
placed that special emphasis on each word of
the sentence.

Ladies and Gentlemen, the prosecution rests.

In psychology and cognitive science, confir-
mation bias is a tendency to search for or inter-
pret new information in a way that confirms
one's preconceptions and avoids informa-

tion and interpretations that contradict prior beliefs.

"You've made me into a cartoon wife," she tells him. "I am not a cartoon wife."

The Buddha named his son Rahula, which means "fetter."

The Buddha left his wife when his son was two days old. He would never have attained enlightenment if he'd stayed, scholars say.

As for us, our days are like grass.

"We don't know, but the cards know," her daughter says when they are playing a game later.

Are you going to leave him? Is he going to leave you? Do you think you'll make it?

It is her married friends that ask these questions. The single ones don't. They think it's simpler. Sometimes the wife cries. Sometimes she shrugs.

The cards know.

35

The wife has never not wanted to be married to him. This sounds false but it is true.

She has wanted to sleep with other people, of course. One or two in particular. But the truth is she has good impulse control. That is why she isn't dead. Also why she became a writer instead of a heroin addict. She thinks before she acts. Or more properly, she thinks *instead* of acts. A character flaw, not a virtue.

Do you have a secret life? This is what she asks all her friends. Hardly any of the other writers do. But a few people avert their eyes before answering. No, they say. Either that or they tell her everything.

She has never had a secret life. But after all of this, she does a little. But the secret part seems too small to tell anyone who might be a true secret lifer.

Like how two guys are sending her music, how she is taking yoga, how she has borrowed $400 from the philosopher that she keeps hidden in an envelope in the closet, how she has received but not cashed her royalties check.

"Sometimes I think of revenge," she tells him. He winces. "What would that look like?"

In Africa, they tied the couple together and threw them into a river of crocodiles.

In ancient Greece, the punishment was a root vegetable inserted into the anus.

In France, the woman was made to chase a chicken through the streets naked.

Door #3?

How did you meet? Go back to the beginning.

This is what the worksheet in the adultery book says.

It will be a long time before one of the Voyagers *will encounter another star. And even then it won't come very close. There is a red dwarf star called Ross 248. In 40,000 years,* Voyager 2 *will come within 1.7 light-years of it, still far enough away that it will seem like no more than a dot of light. Astronomers say that if you looked at it through the porthole of* Voyager 2, *it would seem to slowly brighten over the millennia, then slowly dim for many more.*

There is one thing the wife tells the philosopher which she isn't sure anyone else will understand. If she tells it to someone else, they might think she is being self-deprecating. But she isn't being self-deprecating. She is being religious. The thing is this: Even if the husband leaves her in this awful craven way, she will still have to count it as a miracle, all of those happy years she spent with him. "It was a fucking miracle that I found him," she tells the philosopher. "A fucking miracle. Past tense." They are sitting cross-legged on the floor like they used to in their dorm rooms. "I think I was afraid to go all in," she says.

"Because all in is terrifying. With all in, you lose everything." He nods and suddenly they are both crying a little.

He calls her up later. "Get him up to the country. You can leave him in six months if you want, but get him out of here."

The adultery book says it's unwise to make any big moves in the aftermath of such an event. *There is, unfortunately, no geographical cure.*

Bullshit, her sister says.

She goes to visit her and writes the husband a letter from London. She isn't sure if she should use the old return address, but then at the last minute she pencils it in. She is after all, speculating.

Dear Husband,
Forget the city. There is nothing for us anymore.
The birds are leaving even. I saw two pigeons on
the runway when my plane took off yesterday.

She'll leave the city to her students, the ones whose shoes are held together by electrical tape, the ones who tear up at the sight of discarded umbrellas, the ones who buy the inscrutable Russian candy and the halal goat meat. Just last week, one was outside her office memorizing all the categories of clouds (in case this proved necessary).

"What is the worst thing that ever happened to him?" her sister asks her. And the answer is nothing ever has.

"That's the problem," she says. "He's just a nice boy from Ohio. He has no idea how to fix something like this."

There is a pause and the wife thinks they are both wondering what it would be like to grow up like that. Their mother died when they were young. Their father was elsewhere. What would it be like to make it so late into life before trouble hit? To always have someone on the front porch, calling you to dinner? The husband doesn't have even a touch of this raised-by-wolvesness.

But the girl does, she bets. Something in her past that makes her want to tear things to shreds.

Is it possible there is some alternate universe in which the wife and the girl would be friends? She has heard such stories before from her grad students, of the sad-seeming married man, of the unkind wife, of the "all I did was send him music" variety.

She imagines having lunch with her and hearing the story of this married guy she thinks she's in love with. Should she get him drunk and say something? She is almost positive he feels the same. The way he looks at her, the way they walk back together from lunch, their hands almost touching.

What Ann Druyan said: *Compressed into a minute-long segment, the brain waves of a woman newly in love sound like a string of firecrackers exploding.*

Recent Posts

Why do we age?
Where is the best place to live?
Which rules are right?
Do aliens exist?

There are many ways in which she has been a good wife, some that would hold up under cross-examination even. But when she thinks of listing them, she keeps hearing the voice of a TV lawyer in her head.

No special pleading is what he says.

36

Even the stars look different now. The girl is outdoorsy, the husband has told her. The wife keeps imagining the two of them going camping in the mountains. How he'd name the constellations one by one, the girl alert in her softest sweater, nodding, looking up at all that sky.

The adultery book says to say affirmations of some sort each day, about yourself or your marriage. The wife doesn't like the ones that are suggested so she makes up her own.

Nerves of Steel
No favors for fuckers

The wife tries to repeat this to herself in the morning as she brushes her teeth. Sometimes she doesn't manage it. Sometimes she pulls back her lips and looks at her bloodied gums instead.

One day in the Little Theater of Hurt Feelings the husband announces that he would like to try a separation. The wife is stunned. He has said nothing to her until now. But the shrink discourages it. "You might as well just get divorced," she says. Later, the wife remembers that they are supposed to fly to Ohio in two weeks to see his family, the whole blond band of them. "I guess I'll be skipping that trip," she says. "No," the husband tells her. "You should come." She looks at him. "Why would I?" He waves his hand magnanimously. "Because we still are?" Married, he means.

What Rilke said: *I want to be with those who know secret things or else alone.*

A year ago the philosopher's brother died suddenly of an aneurism. He had a wife, no kids. He lived in Colorado and made wooden mailboxes that he sold through a catalog printed on newsprint. The next day, the philosopher flew to the little town where his brother had lived. He went to the lumber store with his sister-in-law and bought pinewood for the coffin. Then in his brother's shop he drew a sketch on cardboard and began. After a few hours, she came out to watch him. He put a blanket around her, made her tea, but he didn't try to make her go in. All night she watched him saw and hammer. We could see our breath, he said.

The wife sends a note to the philosopher at 2:30 in the afternoon. "I am very awake. Are you?"

"Maybe it's you?" she thinks of writing to him.

Some mornings the wife goes to the philosopher's house and sits in his kitchen with him. Together, they come up with a theory of everything. The air feels electrified. She keeps wanting to ask if he can feel it too or if it is just some kind of weather in her head. "Tell me the truth. Do I seem crazy?" she says. He makes her an egg, puts it down in front of her. He pauses for a long time, then shakes his head. "You seem very, very awake," the philosopher says.

She imagines how she would feel at his funeral. How she would feel at the husband's. She puts her hand over her heart for a moment and leaves it there. Yes, still beating.

What Martin Luther said: *Faith resides under the left nipple.*

37

And then there is another fight. "Us," he says about the girl again. The wife leaves in the middle of the night and goes to a hotel. She takes a car across town to a Holiday Inn Express because she can't bear to sleep on anyone's couch, to see husbands, to see children. She watches herself sign the register. She watches herself check in. She wanted him to feel something when he saw the door slam behind her, but did he?

She left without a toothbrush. Without a book. Without sleeping pills even. She has her phone on. He doesn't call her. She texts to say where she is. *In case she needs me* is how she phrases it. Nothing then. Nothing. She waits, watching the door as if it might open. She hears herself making noise, a soft sound, half cry, half croon.

I am in a hotel, she thinks. *In a hotel you can do anything.* Now she goes through every drawer in the room. What is she looking for? A gun? A needle? She shifts from bed to chair to desk, but there is no place that will stop her head.

It is dawn when she goes out into the street again, when she calls a car to get her. The man who picks her up thinks she is a hooker. He smiles at her in the rearview mirror. She says she needs to get home before her daughter wakes up and he speeds through the quiet streets for her.

But it doesn't matter that she returns. He is asleep and when he wakes up he won't even look at her. "You left," he mutters. "You left." A whisper fight and then he is up and dressed. There is something about his eyes that stops her. "You're not thinking of going there, are you?" she asks him. From his face, she sees yes, he is thinking this. For the first time, she plays the unplayable card, her daughter's name. "Leave if you want, but not like this. If you do, you are going to change who she is."

What she means by "like this" is, with your face shaking and your hands trembling and your eyes like a hunted animal. She puts her hand on his shoulder, but he shakes her off of him.

The babysitter comes to take the daughter out of the house. The wife calls the philosopher and he comes right away. She is waiting outside on the street for him and he has to hold her up, keep her from falling. A group of Pakistani men looks on impassively. "Keep him," she pleads. "Just for tonight. Don't let him leave. Promise me."

The philosopher keeps him at his apartment. He doesn't have a couch so he takes the husband to Ikea and they go shopping for an extra bed. It sounds like a sitcom, the wife thinks when she hears this. But where to put the laugh track? At the store while they are trying them out or later at home when they are assembling it?

It is easy in retrospect to see why he'd want to go. There are two women who are furious at him. To make one happy, he must take the subway across town and arrive on her doorstep. To make the other happy, he must wear for some infinitely long period of time a hair shirt woven out of her own hair.

38

Her ex-boyfriend calls her. He says he wants to talk. She meets him on a bench in the park. She has been up all night, thinking, testing out conversations. "You look great," her ex says. "Amazing actually." Everyone has been saying that to her lately. That she looks radiant, glowing. She refuses to mention the yoga. It isn't that. It's that the scrim has fallen away. All right, all right, maybe it's the yoga. It's true that it's hard to work the scrim thing in conversationally. She smiles at him. He sits beside her, their knees almost touching. They talk about little things. He is smart and funny as always and now, incredible bonus, no longer a speed freak. People walk by with their dogs. Leaves fall prettily. The wife alludes to her situation, obliquely at first, then nakedly. As she talks, her ex is looking at her, smiling, laughing, but then suddenly she sees his eyes dart away. It is possible that she is talking too fast, that her hands are shaking. "My heart is like a paper bag," she says. "See?" She sees him register that she is not what he had thought she was. Something crosses his face. Fear? Pity? She forces herself to stop talking. He is twitchy now, ready to leave and go to a meeting, she thinks. "I think I need a sponsor," she says. "That's what everyone says," he tells her. They stand up. Then there is a long walk to the subway. She should take another path, walk another way. Someone else would make an excuse, exit gracefully with a wave. But no, horribly they round the corner, horribly they pass the arch and the benches and the newsstand. "Take care," he says as she lurches oddly away. It hurts her eyes to look at these buildings. Greener, she thinks. There are the trees and the water. The expanse of lawn, overly peopled. She walks through the park, holding herself carefully. There is a sense of being unprotected in an open space. I am at the mercy of the elements, she thinks.

What Kafka said: *I write to close my eyes.*

39

Once ether was everywhere. The crook of an arm, say. (Also the heavens.) It slowed the movement of the stars, told the left hand where the right hand went. Then it was gone, like hysteria, like the hollow earth. The news came over the radio. *There is only air now. Abandon your experiments.*

The wife wants to go to the hospital. But she does not want to have gone to the hospital. If she goes, she might not come back. If she goes, he might use it against her. But when she is alone, the objects around her bristle with intent. This is fascinating to her but it must remain a secret. She packs her daughter's lunches and reads her to sleep. On the playground, she impersonates a reasonable mother watching her child play in a reasonable way. She goes to work, hovers above herself as she speaks about all manner of things. She is as canny as an addict. She covers up when she misspeaks. She goes to the Little

Theater of Hurt Feelings once a week and talks reasonably about the future, but secretly she is squirreling away money in books and journals. She stays up half the night, her brain whirring and whirring. She looks up school calendars in other cities. She investigates the cost of cars, of heat, of health insurance. She makes a plan a, a plan b, a plan c and d and e. Of these, only one involves the husband.

Her sister listens to the story about the coffin. "Okay, remind me again why you never went out with him?" she asks.

"I thought you wanted to be an art monster," the husband says.

The philosopher's sister-in-law ordered a piece of antique mourning jewelry to wear. A gold locket with a place inside to put a picture of the one who died. On the outside there is a small etched rose. But *Prepare to follow* is engraved on the inside of it. The nineteenth century. Jesus. Those people did not mess around.

How was the bake sale?

She sends her best friend a text. "11pm. Husband still playing video games." There is a little ping. The husband looks at her. "You sent that to me."

Her sister is the one who comes up with the winning plan. They should move to her ramshackle house in Pennsylvania and live there for next to nothing. The wife checks the schools. She checks the car insurance. She checks the cost of firewood. She orders beekeeping and chicken-tending books for him and starts filling out forms so they can adopt a puppy when they get there. She fact-checks an eight-hundred-page book about space aviation, then finishes all her grading for school in one fourteen-hour session.

Any flight of ideas?
Any pressured speech?
Any grandiose plans?

Nope.

People who have already moved to the country give warnings: *Beware fracking. Check for ticks. Don't get goats.*

Prepare to follow, the wife thinks. The husband is hardly talking, but he packs the car to the roof and gets in.

They have told the daughter it will take four hours to get there. Every five minutes, she leans forward and asks them again. "Is it an hour? Is it an hour? Is it an hour?" And then they are there.

40

The wife has begun planning a secret life. In it, she is an art monster. She puts on yoga pants and says she is going to yoga, then pulls off onto a country lane and writes in tiny cramped handwriting on a grocery list. She thinks she should go off her meds maybe so as to write more fluidly. Possibly this is not a good idea.

But only possibly.

Fall comes early here. And it is unnerving to see so many stars. At night, the wife lies awake worrying about bears and chimney fires. About the army of spiders that live within. The husband wants goats. The daughter cries for Brooklyn.

The wife keeps finding $20 bills she has stashed away in books. Also tiny pieces of paper she has written on. Here is something she scrawled on the back of a credit card receipt. She squints to read her own handwriting. *I teach immaculately, but lately . . . lately, I've got some dirty windows,* it says.

She can't help thinking about how she has another thing squirreled away in a book. A Monopoly card sent to her by a divorced friend. GET OUT OF JAIL FREE, it says.

But she is tired all the time now. She can feel how slowly she is walking, as if the air itself is something to be reckoned with. The shrink says it's because she has been running on adrenaline until now and that this is starting to recede. "Be careful," she says. "Don't let your mind go to a dark place."

Right, the wife thinks. *Gotcha.* She does not mention how she goes out to look at the sky in the middle of the night. How she stands there in a T-shirt and bare feet, shivering. Witness this wind, this flimsily constructed tree. Theatrical, this terror, she feels.

And everyone drives too slowly here. *Sorry,* the wife thinks as she weaves in and out of lanes. *Sorry, sorry.*

They never talk about it when the daughter is awake. They keep it from her like the bugs, but still it is there under everything, a low hum like furious weather.

One morning she takes her to a playground. The sun beats down on them. "Where is everyone?" the daughter says. She swings listlessly on the monkey bars and then they go home again.

The wife has to remind herself to notice that it is beautiful here. She goes for a walk in the woods after a week of rain, wearing the husband's heavy boots.

The rain has brought the mosquitoes back. The wife unpacks the bug zapper that the almost astronaut gave her. There are still a lot of boxes in the attic. *I should be more efficient,* she thinks. The husband sets up their old telescope. There is almost no light pollution here. The wife looks up at the sky. There are more stars than anyone could ever need.

One day while the daughter is at school, the husband and wife drive to a neighboring town to see a movie. On the way there, they pass a Holiday Inn Express. The wife stiffens. "What?" he says. She points to it. "I spent the worst night of my life in one of those." The husband looks at her blankly. "In a Holiday Inn Express?" They drive a little farther. He reaches over and takes her hand. It seems they have taken a wrong turn somewhere because there are farms on either side now, not businesses. The wife looks out the window. A dog runs through the field, his dark fur ruffled with light.

41

The wife is trying not to look at the husband with a cold eye, but suddenly it is hard not to notice how Midwestern he is. How charmed he is if they do anything wholesome together as a family, like play a board game, how educational he wants all of their outings with the daughter to be. One weekend, they go to some underground caverns and she listens to him go on to the daughter about the composition of limestone. *Class dismissed,* she thinks.

That night, the wife gets up and goes to sleep in her daughter's room. If he asks, she can lie and say she called for her.

Fight or flight, she thinks. *Fight or flight.*

She has noticed though that he seems to love her again. A little at least. He is always touching her now, brushing the hair back from her face. "Thank you," he says one night as they are sitting in the yard. He says it was as if they were all trapped under a car and in a burst of inexplicable strength, she moved it. He kisses her and there is something there, a flicker maybe, but then she hears the bug zapper going. *Zzzft. Zzzft. Zzzft.* "You shouldn't have driven us off of the cliff," she says.

42

The wife braids the daughter's hair every morning before school. At bedtime, the husband reads to her from *Anne of Green Gables*.

They are both worried about the daughter. At night, she writes long letters to her favorite doll, then mails them in a Kleenex box she keeps hidden under her bed.

If they ask the daughter why she is crying, she says, "Don't talk about it."

The husband decides to teach the daughter how to whistle and the wife listens to them in the backyard whistling away.

The wife still has a plan b just in case. *I could join the Amish,* she thinks whenever they pass them.

For the daughter's birthday, they decide to get her a puppy. She is ecstatic, but it does the final work of unhinging the wife. "Can you take it back?" the shrink says more urgently than expected. "Take it back!" "No," the wife says. It is the only thing that makes the girl happy. "You'll have to crate it," she says. "Often."

Sometimes the husband says he is going to look for kindling. But later the wife sees him chain-smoking at the edge of the far field.

Sometimes she still thinks about the ex-boyfriend, but she does not hunt for him in the ether.

One morning the wife takes the puppy out for a walk. He blazes ahead then returns covered with burrs. She picks them off and lets him go again. Sky here. She had forgotten how much sky there could be. When she catches up with the puppy, he is eating something dead. "Leave it!" she says. "Leave it! Leave it!" He drops it on the ground, wags his tail at her. But later, the puppy runs back to the same place and rolls around in it.

Don't drink. Don't think.

The wife and the husband take the puppy to the vet to get his shots. They pass the Holiday Inn Express again. This time she manages not to say anything. She feels him notice this. After a while, he turns on the radio. The puppy licks the steering wheel. To their surprise, he is well behaved at the vet. He doesn't pee on the floor or nip at the hand that holds him. But later when they get home, he stands on his hind legs and drinks from the toilet.

That night the wife can't stop her hands from flapping. She goes out into the dark field to get away. But the daughter sees her and follows. "Mommy!" she says. "Mommy! Where are you going?"

So she takes the pills the doctor gives her. Her hands stop flapping. She is less inclined to lie down in the street. But her brain is still buckling. In the parking lot of a store two towns over she cries like a clown with her face on the steering wheel.

43

The wife has a little room now, one that looks out over the garden. She makes a note to herself about the book she is writing. *Too many crying scenes.*

One day the husband sees a woodchuck looking through the window at them. It is with great joy that they discover that another name for this creature is "the whistle pig."

The daughter has stopped talking so much about going home. She is building something in the far corner of the yard now. They watch as she carries heavy rocks across the grass and dumps them in a pile. Days pass, but the construction remains mysterious. Sometimes she changes her mind and moves everything a few feet to the right or left. It seems to be some kind of game. "Backyard Gulag," they call it.

The husband and wife whisper-fight now in the gloves-off approved way. She calls him a coward. He calls her a bitch. But still they aren't that good at it yet. Sometimes one or the other stops in the middle and offers the other a cookie or a drink.

And then one day the wife realizes she's driven past the Holiday Inn Express without noticing. Maybe it's becoming just a hotel again. Not the place where she stood, then sat, then knelt, palms turned down on the bed-spread. *Dear God, Dear Monster, Dear God, Dear Monster,* she prayed that night, shaking like a junkie until the slow sun rose again.

What Rilke said: *Surely all art is the result of one's having been in danger, of having gone through an experience all the way to the end, to where no one can go any further.*

44

I'm hungry. I want to eat something delicious, have a beer and a cigarette. I've come back to Earth full of desires. The air tastes good.

This is what the Japanese reporter said when he came back from the space station.

In the morning, the wife lets the dog out: *Hey a squirrel! Hey a tree! Hey a piece of shit! Hey! Hey! Hey!*

They bathe him together, toweling him off gently. Afterwards, the wife gives him peanut butter and watches him lick it from the spoon.

What Emily Dickinson said: *Existence has overpowered Books. Today I slew a Mushroom.*

The husband buys a grand piano. No one out in the country cares how long or loud he plays. He teaches the daughter a few finger exercises. But she would rather pack a bag of candy and climb a tree.

He composes something beautiful for the wife. *Songs About Space*, he calls it. Sometimes she plays it late at night when he is asleep. She thinks of that radio show, wonders if the girl still listens to it.

For a long time, the wife had an idea that the girl might write her a letter. But, no, no, of course, there is nothing.

The wife sits in the backyard with binoculars. She is trying to learn about the birds. She has seen robins and sparrows and wrens. A green-throated hummingbird. She wants to know the name of the black bird with the red wings. She looks it up. It is a red-winged blackbird.

Dear Girl,

She writes the philosopher a letter instead. He has gone to live in the Sonoran Desert.

He met a poet there who tends sixty kinds of cacti and speaks three languages. *Yes,* the wife says. *Stay.* She tells him about the red-winged blackbird because it is important to know the names of things.

My brother used to ask the birds to forgive him; that sounds senseless, but it is right.

The leaves are nearly gone now. The daughter is pressing them into a book. The husband is outside chopping wood.

(So ask the birds at least. Ask the fucking birds.)

45

The weather is theater here. They watch it through the window from their bed.

What Singer said: *I wonder what these people thought thousands of years ago of these sparks they saw when they took off their woolen clothes?*

The husband feeds the stove so she can stay in bed. He goes outside to get more wood. The sky looks like snow, he says.

Saint Anthony was said to suffer from a crippling despair. When he prayed to be freed from it, he was told that any physical task done in the proper spirit would bring him deliverance.

At dinner, the wife watches the husband as he peels an apple for the daughter in a perfect spiral. Later, when she is grading papers, she comes across a student's story with the same image in it. The father and daughter, the apple, the Swiss Army knife. Uncanny really.

Beautifully written. She checks for a name, but there is nothing. Lia, she thinks. It must be Lia. She goes outside to read it to the husband. "I wrote that," he says. "I slipped it into your papers to see if you would notice."

The Zen master Ikkyu was once asked to write a distillation of the highest wisdom. He wrote only one word: *Attention*.

The visitor was displeased. "Is that all?"

So Ikkyu obliged him. Two words now. *Attention. Attention.*

Sometimes the wife still watches him sleep.

Sometimes she still strokes his hair in the middle of the night and half asleep he turns to her.

Their daughter runs through the woods now, her face painted like an Indian.

What the rabbi said: *Three things have a flavor of the world to come: the Sabbath, the sun, and married love.*

46

Snow. Finally. The world looks blankly beautiful. We take the dog out in it. He races ahead of us, blazing a trail of pee through the whiteness. We walk towards the road. Sometimes the school bus is early, sometimes late. There is ice in the trees, a brisk, bitter wind from the east. The dog appears, dragging his leash. We wait by the mailboxes. One or two trees still have some leaves. You reach out to pick one, show it to me. "It has oblique leaves," you say. "See?" I let you tuck it in my pocket.

The yellow bus pulls up. The doors open and she is there, holding something made of paper and string. It is art, she thinks. Science maybe. The snow is coming down again. Soft wet flakes land on your face. My eyes sting from the wind. Our daughter hands us her crumpled papers, takes off running. You stop and wait for me. We watch as she gets smaller. No one young knows the name of anything.

ACKNOWLEDGMENTS

Many thanks to the Ucross Foundation, Ledig House, NYFA, and Ellen Levine Fund for giving me the space and time to write this book.

I am immensely grateful to Joshua Beckman, Lydia Millet, Rob Spillman, Elissa Schappell, Tasha Blaine, Michael Rothfeld, Merrie Koehlert, Greg Koehlert, Helen Phillips, Adam Thompson, Jon Dee, Steve Rhinehart, Fred Leebron, Liz Strout, Josh Glenn, Alex Abramovich, Mike Greer, Sam Lipsyte, Ceridwen Morris, Dorla McIntosh, Rebecca Leece, Laura Ogden, Bethany Lyttle, Ben Marcus, Ethan Nosowsky, Michael Cunningham, Matthea Harvey, Tom Hart, Leela Corman, Lucy Raven, Mimi Lipson, Anna DeForest, Aaron Retica, Sarah Bassett, Anstiss Agnew, Caroline Bleeke, Evalena

Leedy, Joshua Henkin, and Sam Fox for their generosity and encouragement in matters literary and far beyond.

Thanks to my agent, Sally Wofford-Girand, who stood by me all these years and knew just when to wrench this thing out of my hands, as well as to my editor, Jordan Pavlin, whose thoughtful notes made this book much better than it was.

Above all, I want to thank my family whose love and support are the foundation of everything good and true in my life.

And to the crackerjack editorial, publicity, and production staff at Knopf who shepherded this maddeningly formatted book to press, I owe each and every one of you a pony.

A NOTE ABOUT THE AUTHOR

Jenny Offill is the author of the novel *Last Things,*
which was chosen as a Notable Book of the Year by
The New York Times and was a finalist for the L.A.
Times First Book Award. She is the coeditor, with
Elissa Schappell, of two anthologies of essays, *The
Friend Who Got Away* and *Money Changes Every-
thing.* Her children's books include *17 Things I'm
Not Allowed to Do Anymore, 11 Experiments That
Failed,* and *Sparky.* She teaches in the writing pro-
grams at Queens University, Brooklyn College, and
Columbia University.

A NOTE ON THE TYPE

Pierre Simon Fournier *le jeune,* who designed the type used in this book, was both an originator and a collector of types. His services to the art of printing were his design of letters, his creation of ornaments and initials, and his standardization of type sizes. In 1764 and 1766 he published his *Manuel typographique,* a treatise on the history of French types and printing, and on what many consider his most important contribution to typography—the measurement of type by the point system.

Typeset by Scribe, Philadelphia, Pennsylvania
Printed and bound by RR Donnelley,
Crawfordsville, Indiana
Designed by Iris Weinstein